Raves For the Work of GIL BREWER!

"[One] of the most adroit plot-spinners of the paperback era."
—*Geoffrey O'Brien, Hardboiled America*

"Gil Brewer has spent a long time in the shadows of his more famous contemporaries, but his best work—a noir blend of James M. Cain, Dashiell Hammett and Ernest Hemingway—gives his rivals a run for their money. I'm delighted to see him making a comeback."
—*Allan Guthrie*

"There is a Woolrichian darkness and desperation in his best work. It stays with you a long, long time."
—*Mickey Spillane & Max Allan Collins,*
A Century of Noir

"The prose is lean [yet] rich with raw emotion genuinely portrayed and felt."
—*Bill Pronzini*

"A short but full-packed story, pointed and restrained… an effective tale of an ordinary man trying to turn sharpie and destroying himself in the process."
—*Anthony Boucher, The New York Times*

"One of the most respected (and collected) of the Gold Med……"

She pouted. "Please. I'd like a fire."

She had the blankets spread all around the floor in front of the fireplace. I dumped the wood in a box, and set the fire with some old newspapers underneath the wood. It caught quickly, and the room became a chimera of fire and shadow.

When I turned around, she was naked, lying there on the blankets.

"Get the money, Jack."

I didn't say anything. I got the money bag and brought it back.

"Pour it out," she said. "Here." She slapped the blanket between us.

I opened the bag and turned it upside down. The money fell there on the blanket between us, piling up and piling up. I threw the small suitcase across the room, and knelt looking at it.

"It kind of makes you crazy," I said. "Doesn't it?"

"Undress," she said. "Like me. Take your shirt off."

The firelight was high now, and the flames danced across the ceiling and played like thin wicked fingers across the pile of money.

"Jesus, Jack—just look at it, will you?"

I felt a little crazy, right then. I couldn't help it.

Shirley knelt by the money. She reached into it with both fists and tossed it into the air, and watched it flutter down. I lay there, watching her. She was beautiful, Christ, they didn't come any more beautiful than Shirley Angela. Kneeling there with that big pile of money, and the firelight playing across her body, breasts, hip and thigh, her flesh sheened a little with perspiration from the heat so it mirrored the flames—there was never anything like it...

The Vengeful
VIRGIN

by **Gil Brewer**

A HARD CASE CRIME NOVEL

A HARD CASE CRIME BOOK

(HCC-030)

First Hard Case Crime edition: April 2007

Published by

Titan Books
A division of Titan Publishing Group Ltd
144 Southwark Street
London
SE1 0UP

in collaboration with Winterfall LLC

Print edition ISBN 978-0-85768-374-8
E-book ISBN 978-0-85768-387-8

Cover design by Cooley Design Lab
Design direction by Max Phillips
www.maxphillips.net

Typeset by Swordsmith Productions

The name "Hard Case Crime" and the Hard Case Crime logo are trademarks of Winterfall LLC. Hard Case Crime books are selected and edited by Charles Ardai.

Printed in the United States of America

Visit us on the web at www.HardCaseCrime.com

THE VENGEFUL VIRGIN

One

She wasn't what you would call beautiful. She was just a red-haired girl with a lot of sock. She stood behind the screen door on the front porch, frowning at me.

"I'm Jack Ruxton," I said. "From Ruxton's TV. Sorry I'm late."

"That's all right."

She was maybe seventeen or eighteen. The porch light was on. It was about eight o'clock on a Monday night. Looking past her, I could see through a long, broad living room, expensively furnished, and on into a brightly lighted bedroom. A man with iron-gray hair lay on a hospital bed under a sheet, with his toes sticking straight up. His head was flung back as if he were in a cramp. There was a lot of tricky-looking paraphernalia, rubber hoses and tanks and stuff, beside the bed. A fluorescent bedlight glared across his face. It was eerie.

"Well," I said. "TV on the blink?"

"No. That's not what I called you for, Mr. Ruxton."

She caught on that it was uncomfortable with the screen door between us, gave it a shove with her knee. I backed away on the porch. She stepped out and closed the door.

"I'm Shirley Angela," she said.

I nodded. She had on a red knitted thing, made of one piece. It was shorts and a top, without sleeves. The top was what I think they call a boat-neck, tight up against her throat. The whole thing was very tight on her. Her face seemed almost childlike, but she was no child.

She said, "Let's go out back and talk."

"Okay."

"He's sleeping. He only sleeps a few minutes. It might wake him if we went in now."

"Okay."

She brushed past me and walked down the sloping cement ramp built from the top of the porch to the front walk. There were no steps. The ramp was for wheelchair cases. I followed her.

The hair was shoulder length, and more auburn, close up. Her waist was extremely narrow. She walked on the balls of her feet, throwing her hips out in back. It was there to be looked at, and she must have known it.

"Out here, Mr. Ruxton."

I grunted, and we came around the side of the house on a path of stepping stones. She could really do things on stepping stones. She flipped a switch on a pine tree, and floodlights came on out in the yard. We walked along that way, playing Indian, to where the path ended. She paused, but didn't turn, and said, "There are just the two of us living here. I have to take care of everything." Then she moved off again.

I didn't say anything.

The lot was a big one, maybe two hundred by three hundred. It was wooded with Australian pine, a couple of big old water oaks, and royal palms. You could see soft lights in a house beyond a hedge next door. There was a sea wall down there by the Gulf, and the moon and floodlights gleamed on the water. Three weathered lawn chairs stood around a rusting steel-topped table that had once been white.

"We can sit out here."

"Okay."

We moved the chairs away from the table and sat.

I didn't know what we were waiting for, but neither of us said anything for a minute or two. You knew she was young, yet there was something contained about her. She was almost serene. Her skin was pale, almost pure white. Her face was smooth and oval, but with high cheekbones under the velvety skin. Looking at her, you knew it would be something to lay your hands on that soft white skin; very smooth, like a breast, all over.

The thought did occur to me: What the hell is she doing here alone with that old guy in the bed? And somehow I knew it wasn't any money problem. That's all I thought, though. I decided to let her carry the ball, and quit thinking how good she looked. Grace had looked good, too, and now she had me half nuts, the way she was acting. We had had it good and then lost it, and now she wouldn't let me alone and I couldn't shake her. It made me half sick every time I thought of Grace. I didn't know what the hell to do about her.

"Florida's sure nice, nights like this," I said. "That's a fine breeze. Smell the salt?"

"Mr. Ruxton. It's really going to entail a lot of work —what I want done."

Her voice was much like her face. It seemed kind of flat and childish at first, until the overtones hit you. She leaned forward and spoke earnestly. "We have only one television set, a small one. One of these cheap seventeen-inch portable models. It's just no darned good, what with those dog ears they use."

"Rabbit ears," I said. "If the set's any good, you should have decent reception. Of course, out here on the beaches, you might have some interference. I'll check into that."

"Yes. But what we want are two large sets. Color. One for the living room, and then I want one suspended over his bed, so he can watch it in bed, you see?"

"Hm-m-mmm."

"He's able to get up, of course, when he feels well. But mostly he's in bed, lately. It would be best to hang it right over his head. So he could see it easily."

She leaned back and folded her hands in her lap.

"We'd pay cash, of course," she said. "You don't have to worry about that."

"Wasn't worrying."

She smiled briefly.

"Think I can handle everything you want, Miss Angela."

"And, also—a good antenna."

"Okay."

"That's not all. I want one of these intercom businesses set up, too. Between all of the rooms. So he can call me whenever he needs me. Sometimes he needs me in a hurry. His voice isn't too strong."

"We can take care of that."

"I have no idea which brand is best. I used to read these consumers' reports, but I don't keep up anymore. Naturally, Victor—Mr. Spondell, that is—doesn't care, so long as everything works perfectly. He's particular about buying the very best, though."

"I understand."

She was a puzzler. I knew she was in her teens, yet she had that direct and deadly poise of a woman beyond her years.

I was figuring Miss Shirley Angela was going to help my business in her own small way. This looked like a good deal. You've got to whittle every stick you get your hands on, if you expect to be big. Your business has to be the biggest and the best, if you expect it to pay off. That's how it was going to be with me. There was the new annex, and two new trucks, and

two new men. I was plenty in debt. But if you're smart
enough to find all the angles and ride them down, you
won't drown. In the beginning, you've got to scramble,
and you've got to ride those angles hard, every damned
one of them. You don't let any of them throw you, not
even the measliest, because every buck adds up. Either
that, or you make it big and fast some way, and quit
cold. I had learned the hard way, misfiring across a lot
of lousy years, that I would have to slug for it—slug
everybody in sight. So I was glad I'd come out here
myself, instead of sending one of the men from the
shop. It had been mostly by chance, and because
Grace was hanging around again outside the store.

I decided to hold off the pitch till after we were
inside the house. From the way it looked, the guy in
there wouldn't be any hindrance.

Things seemed a little strained, though, and I
wasn't sure why. I kept wondering what her relation-
ship was to the guy in there.

"We can go in now," she said. "He'll be awake."

We walked back the way we had come and went
into the house. As we entered the living room she
said, "I'll let you decide the best place for everything,
Mr. Ruxton. You'll know best, I'm sure."

We left his room until last. She was avoiding it, and
trying every way she knew to make it look as if she
wasn't avoiding it. I wanted to get a good look at him,
and that room. Her acting the way she did only made
it worse. The room was like a magnet.

It was a fairly large house: large living room, three bedrooms, dinette, kitchen, three bathrooms, and a sprawling glassed-in area they call a Florida room down here. It was so quiet you could hear him clear his throat, or change position on the bed.

I couldn't keep my eyes off her legs and she knew it. We were in the kitchen when she excused herself and came back in a minute buttoning up a yellow housecoat.

"What do you think, Mr. Ruxton?"

"Well, there'll be a few minor difficulties in the wiring, but we'll iron them out. Maybe I'd better have a look in there, now."

She turned quickly away. "All right." We went into his bedroom.

"Victor?"

He opened his eyes and stared at me.

"Victor, this is Mr. Ruxton. He's come to put in the TV sets and everything. Like we talked about. He wants to check your room."

He blinked, just once, staring at me. Those blue eyes were really sharp. Somehow they reminded me of an eagle's I'd seen in a Belgian zoo. It was as if he stared at the wall right through your head.

"Good," he said. "That's good."

His voice wasn't strong. He had finely drawn features, a long nose, and heavy brows knotted with snarled gray hair. There was a quality of stubborn arrogance in his glance, of tired determination. The hair on his head was iron-gray, and like barbed wire. He looked as if he were grinning, but it was only the shape of his mouth when relaxed. He wore light gray pajamas. The sheet was neatly drawn and folded across his chest, his hands folded on the sheet. He was a shell, but looked as if he'd once been as strong as an ox.

The sound of his normal breathing was bad. Something like a horse with an advanced case of the heaves.

"Ruxton, eh?" he said, breathing like wind in an October corn field. "The only Ruxton I believe I ever had the pleasure of becoming acquainted with was an unmitigated ass and a dirty son of a bitch. You any relation to him?"

I watched the hands shake; big, once-powerful hands, folded on the sheet.

"Probably," I said.

Some gut-wrung breathless sounds burst past his lips. He was laughing. I knew then I wasn't going to make any pitch to her for anything. I would do my job and get out of here. I didn't like the guy.

"Victor," she said, moving quickly to the side of the bed. "Please, take it easy, will you?"

"Oh, Christ," he said. He spoke with soft pain. She glanced at me, her eyes up-flung in a show of resignation, and began straightening his pillows.

There were oxygen tanks beside the bed, standing upright in a nickel-steel rack with wheels and handles. A long black coil-rubber hose and mask dangled over one side of the gleaming handles like an eyeless phython with its mouth open.

The room was antiseptically clean, neat and white. Not even a magazine or a chair. Just the hospital-type bed and the oxygen tanks. To the left a white-curtained window opened on the side of the house, over the path that led out back. Another window was at the head of the bed. Hanging on a bedpost by a black ribbon was a small, filigreed silver bell; the kind that used to sit on the back of the buffet at your grandmother's house in the long ago of your early childhood.

I stared at the ceiling over the bed, trying to make it look as if I were doing my job. You think about hanging TV sets on the ceiling, only you just don't do it.

"I'll have to check the attic rafters," I said.

"All right," she said.

I looked at him again. He didn't seem too well.

I went over to the bedroom door, and she came along, and we stepped into the living room. The housecoat was coming unbuttoned. She watched my eyes.

"He's very bad off," she said.

"How do I get into the attic? You have a flashlight?"

"Yes—"

The sound reached me faintly from the bedroom. A butterfly brushed a broken wing against the silver bell.

"Shir-*ley!*"

It was Death croaking.

She gave me a quick look and hurried back into the bedroom. I watched her. He writhed on the bed, his mouth open, hands clenching the sheets. He was trying to breathe.

"Would you please help me?" she said.

I went in there.

"Turn that handle wide open. Yes, that's it."

She leaned on him, holding one arm down, and mashed the mask over his nose and mouth and I turned it on. It was life pumping through the rubber hose. I looked away and tried to think of something else so I wouldn't hear him.

In a minute or two she said, "You can turn it off now."

I turned it off. She came around and draped the black rubber hose over the handle. He lay there with his eyes closed. Sweat had formed in splotches on his face and hands.

"Thanks, baby," he said. He didn't open his eyes.

She made a soft purring sound in her throat, and moved to the other side of the bed, straightening the sheet. I watched her and she looked up at me. I caught the expression on her face. It told me a lot.

We watched each other across the bed. She knew I'd seen what she was thinking. It was as if the bed were suddenly empty. He just wasn't there.

She jerked her gaze away and walked out into the living room. I followed, seeing his feet sticking straight up under the sheet, from the corner of my eye. I'd once done apprentice work for an undertaker and had seen a lot of feet like that.

"Sorry you had to see him that way," she said.

"Forget it. Glad to help. Where's that flashlight?"

She went to the kitchen and returned with a five-cell job. I stood on a chair and swung up into the attic through the closet in her bedroom. I checked the rafters. I couldn't get him out of my head. He was just like a corpse, only he still breathed and he was still king.

I came back down.

"Sure," I said, handing her the flashlight. "It won't be too difficult, fastening a TV set to the ceiling."

"I suppose you're still concerned about what happened, aren't you, Mr. Ruxton. I shouldn't've asked you to help. I know how disturbing something like that can be, seeing it for the first time. I just forgot, I'm so used to it."

I thought, Honey, you'll never be used to that.

She must have seen something in my eyes. She spoke quickly. "It's a respiratory ailment. Very complicated. It gets more complicated all the time." She stared toward his room. "Degeneration," she said. "He's been to the finest specialists in the country. Luckily, he's very wealthy." She looked at me again. "It's his lungs, his throat, bronchial tubes—and now, his heart, too. He's—we, that is, have lived every-where, but he likes it here best."

"You're his nurse, then."

"He's my stepfather, Mr. Ruxton. But I suppose you could say I was his nurse. I've been taking care of him ever since he sold the business. He manufactured expensive furniture. All kinds. Surely you've heard the name Spondell? Very likely some of the television cabinets you sell were designed by Victor."

His name might as well have been Xshdkgteydh, for all I'd ever heard of him. I said, "Yeah. The name does seem to ring a bell, at that." She didn't speak, so I said, "How old are you, anyway?"

She looked at me along her eyes. "Eighteen." She paused. "He insisted I take care of him—like this."

"Shouldn't he be in a hospital?"

She gave a little jerk with her head, and sighed. "That's just it. The doctors think so. And now Doctor Miraglia claims it's very important. Victor just tells him 'Bosh!' and refuses to go."

"Who's this Miraglia?"

"He's Victor's doctor now. Victor won't let anyone else come near him. He thinks Doctor Miraglia's the finest doctor in the world." She sighed again. "Everybody thinks Victor should be in the hospital."

"Who's everybody?"

"I mean, before we came here."

"What do you think?"

She smiled. It didn't mean a thing to me, because she'd pushed the whole business much too far. You get to meet a lot of people, and you know how they react when you first meet them. There was only one reason why she'd tell me all this. Maybe two reasons, but I figured I was crazy, thinking the other one. She said, "Let's discuss something else. This must be tiresome to you."

"No relatives?"

"What?"

"Him. Hasn't he any family of his own? I mean, other than you?"

She turned and moved to a broad cocktail table beside a long, low pale blue couch. She laid the flashlight on the table. "Nope," she said. "Nobody but me." She turned and looked at me, smiling.

"Suppose I drop around tomorrow morning?" I said. "I'll bring some stuff along. We can decide what you want. How's that?"

"All right. That's fine."

"If we started anything tonight, we'd never get finished."

"I suppose you're right."

We walked across the room. I stepped out onto the front porch. I looked back at her through the screen.

"Good night, Miss Angela."

"Good night, Mr. Ruxton."

Two

I had that feeling you get. Just a little tight in the chest. Not quite enough air. But so far it was one of those things. I thought again how sometimes I looked too hard at people, trying to figure what made them itch the way they did.

I drove past the store. Somebody had locked up, and only the night lights were on, with the two TV sets in the show window grinding away; one a Western, the other the fights. I always figured, you get them looking in from outside, maybe one or two will drift inside, and you're that much closer to their pocketbooks. I left the sets on all night, because maybe somebody would come back in the morning. Then, sometimes I'd stick around till midnight.

I turned up the alley and drove slowly past the shop. Louis Sneed was at the front bench, working on his hi-fi speaker system, the one he claimed would revolutionize the audio world and cancel out all previous speaker system designs.

I parked the truck in the parking area, lining it up carefully with the other beside me. One truck was out on call, apparently. Twenty-four hour service, that's what. All this so you could stay comfortably in debt at the end of every week, with money in your pocket that wasn't yours, because you had to float it big to make it pay off big someday.

I looked across at the back of the building, at the shop. Big my foot. It was penny ante.

Someday, sweetheart.

I went over to my car, walking quietly. It would be just like Grace to hide on the floor by the back seat. It was okay, she wasn't there. I got in and drove home.

There was no sign of Grace anywhere. I drove once around the block before pulling into the apartment garage, but the streets were quiet. She wasn't hanging around the front of the building, either.

I went on up and took a shower, then mixed a drink. I kept thinking about this Shirley Angela, and how she looked, and how she'd run off at the mouth.

Young and tender.

I went to bed.

In the middle of the night, the phone kept ringing. I got up. It was after three. It was Grace. She'd been drinking and she was crying. She wanted to make sure I knew she was crying.

"I've got to see you, Jack."

"No."

"This isn't fair. It's awful, what you're doing. Don't treat me this way. It isn't fair. It isn't fair."

"Go sleep it off, Grace."

"Please, Jack. Let me come up?"

I hung up and went back to bed. I was half nuts

for morning to come so I could get out to Shirley Angela's place again.

Next morning I hung around the store till ten, getting ready. Pete Stallsworth finally helped me load a couple TV sets on the truck; an RCA console, and a Philco table model for hanging over the bed. I worked up some ideas for brackets, and told Pete I was doing something for a good friend and would handle the whole deal myself. I took along a lot of junk—pamphlets, consumers' reports, pictures, room layouts, good come-on stuff. Why the hell it is, I don't know, but customers always insist on having a mob of phony literature, all glossed up in technicolor. The set itself doesn't matter, it's the folders and pamphlets and crap that really count. Then they hardly look at them.

On the way, I stopped off at Timothy's Radio Supply and signed for four different kinds of intercom units, and told the guy he'd probably have a nice sale on his hands. I drove past the front of the house slowly. It looked different in daylight. Just a house, with palm trees out front, and St. Augustine grass, and the sloping ramp leading to the front porch.

Well, I could be wrong.

I turned in the drive and parked under a tree. The Australian pine hedge between the drive and the neighboring house ran from out back clear to the street. Everything was quiet. I felt low. I had planned to do this whole job myself. It meant carrying TV sets, putting up an antenna, wiring, the works. It wouldn't be easy.

"Hello, there."

"Hi."

She was on the porch, waving.

It didn't make me feel any better, seeing her. I couldn't get it out of my head; something like that, doing what she was doing, prisoned for Christ only knew how long with an old bastard who wouldn't die.

"Morning," I said. "How's everything?"

"Fine."

She was really a knockout this morning. She had on a pair of black toreador pants, skin tight, with little slits at the calf. On top she had somehow managed to squeeze into a thin white sleeveless sweater, so nobody could possibly miss what she had up there. She had plenty. She wore sandals, and a bright smile. Her hair was auburn, all right, and brushed to a sheen.

She came off the porch and around front and along the drive.

"I was expecting you earlier. I phoned, but they told me you'd left."

"I wish now I'd come earlier."

That didn't get me anywhere.

"I'm very anxious to get started," she said. "It's like Christmas—buying all these things."

I got out of the truck and came around to where she stood. I opened the door and hauled the loose-leaf notebooks and the carton of pamphlets off the seat.

She said, "I suppose I could have come down to the store. Doctor Miraglia comes twice a week. That's when I go out to shop, and everything."

"I see." I didn't ask her what "everything" was.

"But I like it this way," she said. "If it's not too much trouble for you."

"Well?"

"Well."

I grinned and nodded toward the house, and she nodded, and started walking that way. I followed her inside. "We can check through this stuff first," I said as we entered the living room. "You can kind of make up your mind. Then we'll get down to brass tacks."

"Swell."

The bedroom door was closed. But I could see him in there, in my mind's eye, staring bleakly into the past....

"Good morning, Ruxton."

Something stopped ticking inside me for a second, then started again. It was Spondell. He stood in the dinette, staring at me with those eagle's eyes. He had on a blue corduroy bathrobe and slippers, and his hair was combed. He held a cup of coffee.

"Well," I said. "Glad you're feeling better."

He started to say something, but she jumped in

fast with the lifeline. "Victor, you'd better toddle back to bed, now. You've been up over a half hour. You know what Doctor Miraglia said."

"The hell with him."

"Now, Victor."

"All right, baby." He grinned. "Glad to see you, Ruxton—you old son of a bitch."

"Victor!"

He had already turned away. He set the coffee cup on the dinette table and walked on through the room to the bedroom door without looking at us. He opened the door and went through and closed it.

"I'm sorry," she said.

I went over to the couch and sat down, and put the carton and the loose-leaf notebooks on the floor.

"He says things like that to everybody," she said. "He seems to think it's funny."

"Gave me a jolt, seeing him."

She came over by the couch, speaking quietly. "I think he tries to prove he's strong by talking like that. He hasn't been quite right—mentally—for some time. I hate to say it, but I think he's getting worse. He was always very sharp. He still is, but he says and does crazy things, sometimes. It worries me."

She was at it again. Telling me her business. I decided to go along with it. "You told his doctor?"

"No." She hesitated. "He'll pay for staying up on his feet, like that. He shouldn't be up at all. But the doctor lets him stay up for ten minutes at a time."

She wanted me to feel sorry for her. "He'll get well."

"No." She was firm. "He'll only get worse and worse."

"Until he dies."

She nodded.

"How long?" I said.

"Hard to tell. It could go on and on."

I didn't say anything for a minute. She looked sad and tired, and she wanted me to know it.

"Sit down," I said. "We'll have a look at this stuff."

Her voice was flat. "It would be a terrible expense if he were in a hospital."

"Thought you said he was wealthy."

"Oh, yes—he is. Very."

"Why would it matter to him, then?"

"It wouldn't matter to him." She paused, then added quickly, "I mean, the expense wouldn't matter. He could practically buy the darned hospital. But he just won't go to a hospital. Not him."

"I see. Well—here's some things I'd like you to look at."

She didn't sit on the couch. She went over and dragged up a low chair, placing it at the corner of the couch where I sat. I put the box of literature and junk on the cocktail table. She kept watching me. She didn't give a good goddamn about that literature.

"I was thinking," she said. "You'll need some sort of remote control. One of those cords, with the gadget on it. So he can work the TV from bed."

"Thought of that."

"Oh. Swell."

"I brought along a couple of TV sets. But first, I'd like you to glance through these folders—ask any questions you want. Oh, by the way, I can give you a good allowance on your old set."

"I thought I'd just stick that in the kitchen."

"I see. A set in every room, to keep you occupied."

"That's what I thought. It gets so—" She shrugged.

She cupped one hand over her brow, looking down at a colorful folder in her lap. I couldn't see her eyes. She didn't say anything, staring down at the folder. Then I saw something. It jarred me. She was only pretending to look. It was a Westinghouse electric kitchen range showing on the folder. The TV blurbs were on the other side.

"That one's a real hot seller," I said. "We call it our oven-grille special."

She didn't move. Then, slowly, she turned the folder over and looked at the other side. She kept the hand cupped over her brow. I still couldn't see her eyes. It was playing it close, but she wasn't fighting it worth a damn. Eighteen years old, I thought. The nipples of her breasts showed through the thin white sweater.

I looked across at the bedroom door. It was closed

but it was still nearby. Too near. I wondered what he was doing in there? Maybe playing leap-frog with his oxygen tanks.

"Wonder if I could have a glass of water?" I said.

She stood up fast. The folder fell to the floor.

"I'm sorry. I should have offered you a drink. I hardly ever drink, you see. It always makes me crazy. I do crazy things. I always seem to lose my head."

"Water will be fine."

Her eyes looked different from the way they had looked a moment before. Something passed between us—something direct and hot.

She turned and walked toward the kitchen, not making a sound, and I watched the way she moved, liking every bit of it. I picked up the folder and dropped it on the table and went out there.

I could walk softly, too. But not that softly. She made as if she didn't hear me. She had the refrigerator door open. I went over beside her and looked at her and she stood there, holding the door, with one hand moving slowly in toward the water bottle. I caught the hand and it crawled up my arm. I put my other arm around her, and she came up against me, watching me with big round eyes, and I kissed her.

She made a small sound and said, "No."

"What the hell do you want?" I said.

Then I thought for a second she was crying. She couldn't be crying. I kissed her again.

I went nuts for her. Her lips were hot. Her mouth

opened, full of tongue. She wormed her body against me, working her hips hard and fast, and began making little frantic sounds in her throat. I'd been right, there was nothing under the white sweater.

She drew her face away. Her eyes were clenched shut. Her lips were stretched back across her teeth with what looked like pain.

"Hold me harder."

If I did that I'd snap her back.

She made a purring sound in her throat. "He's asleep. He won't wake up right now. The door—lock the kitchen door."

I turned and closed and locked it, then held her again. She began to groan and moan, writhing wildly. She was a tiger. She tore at my belt, then began tearing at her clothes, her hair swinging across her face. She yanked her sweater up to her neck and I got as crazy as she was. Those toreador pants of hers were as thin as silk and as tight as skin. They wouldn't come off.

"Rip 'em!"

I ripped. I got my fingers in the seam and ripped the front and left leg practically off. Her flesh was dead white. She dropped to the floor, dragging me with her.

I knew I'd never get enough of her. She was straight out of hell.

Three

I came back to her place at two o'clock, after driving around and trying to think for a little over two hours. She had wanted me to stay for lunch, but I told her I had to get back to the store to take care of orders on electronic equipment. I didn't go near the store. I drove out around Key Causeway and looked at the Gulf of Mexico, and at the light, cloudless sky, and at how brilliant and near-white the sun was up there. All I could think was how she was, with the rest of it a shapeless mass.

There was something about her. She was screwy. I knew that, but I didn't know exactly in what way she was screwy. Not yet. But I thought, Just leave it alone. Get Pete Stallsworth to go out there and finish the installations. Maybe he'll install something personal, too. Only the thought of anybody else with her was bad. Already, it was like that.

I kept thinking about it; what we'd had there on the kitchen floor. How young she was. The soft, smooth feel of her skin, and how hot she was, and the things she said and did. The look of her, lying there, as if she'd die it she didn't get it, maybe.

There had been a lot of women, but never anything like Shirley Angela. And right then I knew I wanted her to be all mine. She made you feel as if you wanted to rape her, because that was the only way you'd get her, reach her. And you had to reach her.

All right. So I was screwy, too. But Shirley Angela was the works.

I drove back and she met me on the porch.

"Did you take care of what you had to take care of?"

"Uh-huh."

We had something between us now, but maybe she wasn't going to admit it was there. They're like that sometimes. You wallow in bed with them all night, and the next day it's, "Good morning, Mr. Ruxton. Would you sign these forms, please? Thank you, Mr. Ruxton."

She kept looking at me. Her eyes were cool.

"I hurried," I said.

She smiled. I began to feel better, because the smile was in her eyes. It was going to be okay.

"How's he doing?" I said.

"Who?"

"Victor. Good old son-of-a-bitching Victor."

We went inside and she closed the door.

"I wish he was dead." She came against me and held on. I kissed her and she pushed away and walked across the living room, and stood by the cocktail table, looking down at the folders and junk I'd left there.

I stood there and looked coldly at her back, and listened in my mind to exactly how she had said that.

I went up behind her and cleared my throat. She moved back against me and pressed, then looked up over her shoulder, smiling. I thrust her away. She turned and looked at me along her eyes.

"I'm wearing a skirt," she said. "See."

"I see."

Her eyes were sly. The skirt was tight and dark blue. She had on a white blouse. She still wore the sandals.

"Would you want a speaker out back, too?" I said. "So it'll cover the yard, in case you're out there?"

She said, "Skirts are better." Then she whispered, "You tore my pants all to hell." She held her right palm against her leg on the skirt and dragged her palm upward. The thin skirt came with it, sliding against the white flesh until her thigh was bare to the hip. "See?"

I began to sweat. "The speaker," I said. "In the back yard."

She spoke normally, holding the skirt up. She moved her hip a little. "I was going to ask you about that, Mr. Ruxton. We may as well do a complete job while we're at it."

"Sure thing." I shot a glance at his bedroom door. The door was closed. I looked back at her and her face had changed. Her expression was bad. She let the skirt fall down.

She turned without looking at me and headed straight for her bedroom, walking as softly as a cat. I followed her. She went into the bedroom and I stepped just inside the door. The room was at the rear of the house, opposite the kitchen. It was all done in pink, with ruffles, and it smelled of her perfume.

She looked at me. "I feel as if I've known you for a long while."

"Yeah."

"I mean it, Jack."

It was the first time she'd called me Jack. No one else had ever said it quite that way, in just that tone of voice.

She sat down at the foot of the bed and leaned against the mahogany bedpost, and wrapped her hands around it, staring at the floor.

"Jack," she said. "I can't stand it." She didn't say anything for a moment, staring at the floor, and neither did I. Then she said, "I've got to talk to somebody about it. It's driving me out of my mind."

I waited. She kept on staring at the floor. There was a tenseness in the very look of her, and it had been revealed in her tone. Whatever it was, she didn't really want to talk about it. You could see her struggle against herself. But she knew she would lose.

"I'm afraid," she said.

Well, I began to really know, then. Before, I'd felt as if I might have read her wrong. Now I was sure about her. It could have been the mailman, the milkman, even Doctor Miraglia. Anybody. Then I thought, No, don't get it wrong. You happened to be here and you saw it in her, and she knows you saw it. Somebody else might have missed it. Only I might never know exactly what it was that had tipped me.

"I'm scared to death, Jack." She stared at the wall, looking toward the other side of the house. "He lies there. He's dying." She paused. I'd been right. She was pulling something up out of her that had been sealed and locked in dark secret compartments for a long time. Every word seemed to be painful. "It goes on and on," she said. "It may go on for years and years. The doctor told me that."

"You've got it pretty soft. Why kick?"

She looked at me and for a second hate shot out of her eyes. Her voice was tight and sibilant. "Soft? For three years I've done this." It was tearing her apart to tell it. But the need was overwhelming. "Three long horrible years. You call that having it soft?"

I shrugged.

"You wonder why I do it," she said. And now the bitterness. "Isn't it obvious?"

I shrugged again.

"Well, isn't it?"

I still didn't speak.

She let go of the bedpost and sat very stiffly. Then she began rocking slightly forward and backward, rubbing her hands tightly against her thighs.

"Why not leave?" I said. "You can get a job."

"No. I can't."

"Why?"

"Because he's leaving me everything when he dies, that's why. All his money. Everything." She swallowed tightly. "He thinks I'm the only friend he's ever had—something. I don't know. It's crazy. I can't leave—I can't."

My throat felt dry. "It won't last forever."

"Any time is forever. Right now is forever the way I feel."

She stood up, staring at me.

I said, "It's a lot of money?"

She pressed both hands against the side of her face and said, "Yes."

"If he were in a hospital, you'd be free. You wouldn't have to worry about this. Only you don't want him in a hospital. Do you."

"No."

"Why, Shirley?"

"I just don't, that's all."

"Yes. But, why?"

"I just don't. Isn't that a good enough reason?"

"No."

"I'll take care of him. I promised."

"No," I said. "That's not the reason. Think, Shirley. Why don't you want Victor Spondell put away in a hospital?"

She tried to speak, but nothing came past her lips. She didn't want to hear herself say it. Her eyes were dark now, the pupils large and black, staring from the strange pallor of her face.

"I'll tell you why," I said. "It's because Victor might live on and on for a long, long time, and you couldn't do anything to prevent it. You couldn't get at him in a hospital. That's why."

She lunged at me and slapped my face. She slapped it again, striking savagely. She was crying, sobbing. I grabbed her wrists and tried to hold her. She fought like a wild Indian.

"It's the truth," I said. "Face it."

"No!"

She wrenched one hand loose and raked her nails down the side of my neck. I grabbed the wrist again and held on. She squirmed and writhed and kicked. Her face was wrung with fright. She was crying inside, but there were no tears in her eyes.

"Get out!" she said. "Get away from me. Leave me alone, you dirty bastard. Get out of here and stay away from me."

I thrust her slowly back toward the bed, fighting with her every inch of the way, and gave her a shove. She landed on her back and lay suddenly still. She looked beautiful to me then, lying there; beautiful and hot and mad.

"All right," I said. "I'll get out."

I turned and walked from the bedroom, across the living room, and out the front door. I closed the screen door gently, then went out to the truck and drove quickly away.

Four

I waited a week. The thought of losing her now had me crazy. I couldn't think of anything but Shirley Angela. Days and nights crawled and crept. It was the longest week I'd ever spent in my life and she was with me every minute in my mind, like a ripe taunt. But if she thought I would run to her, she was wrong. This time she had to come to me. I didn't go near her place. I lashed the tarp over the hoops above the truck-bed, and covered the TV sets and the other stuff inside with a couple of quilts. I told Pete Stallsworth to leave everything just as it was, and not to use that truck, because I was waiting for a call. I prayed she would call.

She was right about time being forever.

Now was forever. My whole life had been forever up until I met Shirley Angela. All the things I'd thought meant something, really meant nothing.

There were the years as a kid on the farm in Louisiana, watching my old man grub and get drunk and thrash around, until the old woman started getting drunk, too, so she could stand it, until he finally ran off with a fat whore who sang "Roll me over, lay me down, and do it again," in a carnival sideshow. And along about then I ran away, maybe emulating my old man, with a girl named Tess who met a slick-haired mulatto in New Orleans and dropped me. Sixteen and mad at everybody. Working at anything I could get, taking anything I could lay my hands on. And then Ginny, making me go back to school, sweet as honey—hit by a truck and killed outright with me watching from the curb, in Memphis. Something happened to me then. I could never figure it. I didn't give a goddamn what happened. I felt mean and low-down. I reckoned I would take the world by the tail and kick it smack in the ass. Only it worked the other way around, all through the years of night school, the war, the drinking and the dames, the brief spell of gas station hoisting, and the cornet blowing in the jive joints, right up to the television school, and finally the store, and Grace. All the time maybe looking for Ginny. I don't know. Maybe thinking I'd found her again in Shirley Angela.

Only knowing I'd found what I really wanted instead.

Because Shirley Angela was for me—she was mine.

Along with something else that was beginning to eat holes in me.

Shirley Angela. Just like that. And all the rest of the love-guff just a mess of words. With me, that's how it was. You either understand or you don't.

If you ever had it like this, you understand.

*

Nothing happened. Over one hundred and sixty-eight hours of complete vacuum, with me riding the hands of the clock. Just holding my breath.

Grace called twice. I hung up on her both times. She worried me. I knew she was priming herself all the time, and eventually something would happen, but I couldn't let myself think about that. Not till I could angle something. Grace had been terrific while it lasted. She was a tall, blonde dish, and she'd been in the process of getting a divorce when I met her one evening at the store. She bought a phonograph. She looked good. We talked ourselves into a date for the next night, and after that things were underway with what you might call a bang.

She would say, "Jack, I've been married for five years. Believe it or not. I feel as if I've been dead all that time."

"You're not dead," I'd say. "Take it from me."

And she would laugh. I didn't realize she was serious, possessive, watchful—suspicious. She was fun. In the beginning. She'd always had enough money, she still had plenty to get along with, even though she didn't tag the ex-husband for alimony. We had a hot time for a while. I told her I went for her in a big way. I was really just trying to make her happy. She didn't know that. I didn't think it mattered.

It mattered.

She began to haunt me. On the phone. At the store. At the apartment. She wanted to be with me every minute. She crawled. About that time, I didn't want to be with her at all. She wasn't fun anymore.

"When you going to ask me to marry you?" she'd say. Only she meant it. It was all she thought of. She was neurotic, searching for the perfect husband-lover-understander. I'd played it all wrong. I told her so. I cursed her. I hit her. Nothing did any good. Sometimes she scared me, the way she acted, the wild things she said.

And lately, the phone calls, stopping me in the street. "I'll kill myself. I mean it, Jack. You can't treat me this way. You love me. You told me you loved me."

Jesus! She'd been married wrong once; she would never learn.

I was at the apartment when the phone rang. I thought it was Grace again. It was Shirley Angela. It was like getting everything you'd ever wanted, all in one lump.

"I phoned the store. They finally gave me your apartment number."

"Don't do that again."

"I've got to see you."

"All right." I tried to sound calm.

"It's four-thirty now. The doctor will be here in a few minutes. I'll come to your place."

"No."

Her voice was strained. "I've got to see you." She paused and I didn't speak, and she said, "You were right, Jack. Of course, you were right."

"Yeah. I've got to go back to the store for a while. I won't be free till six."

"That's a whole hour and a half from now."

"One hundred and sixty-eight and a half hours, total."

Silence.

"That doesn't give me much time," she said. "Doctor Miraglia said he can't stay long tonight."

I made no comment.

"Where shall I meet you?" she said.

"Drive out to Maximo Point, on the bay. Take the boulevard until it bears right. You'll see a brick street to the left. Keep on that till it quits. There's a sulphur spring down there. I'll see you."

"I know the place. Jack, are you angry?"

"No. I was, but I'm not anymore. Are you all right?"

"I will be."

I didn't have to go down to the store, and I couldn't figure what made me tell her that. I wished I hadn't. I wanted to see her so bad I couldn't even think, and if the days had seemed a long while before she called, it was really beginning to stretch now.

I took the car and drove out to Maximo Point and waited. The sun hung low over the Gulf. I was parked by the sea wall under a sprawling live oak, and the late afternoon was quiet, with only the occasional distant scream of a gull. I sat there, more nervous with every minute. I heard a car.

She was driving. It was only a little after five, which

told me the condition I was in. Maybe she had known I didn't have to go to the store. The car was a new Imperial sedan, sleek and black. She rocked it to a stop beside me, ran around, opened the door of my car, and jumped in. She closed the door and sat there.

She looked straight ahead at the windshield, with her chin up a little. I didn't say anything and she didn't look at me. Then she spoke, her voice soft and hesitant and shaded with resignation.

"All right," she said. "You win. You were right."

"What do I win?"

She didn't speak for a moment. Then she said, "It was a shock, having you tell me what I was thinking, like that. To my face."

"You were pretty obvious."

She sat stiffly. "I didn't mean to be."

Looking at her, I felt the lust crawling in me, a kind of liquid heat that spread in my loins. She was soft and eager, and hungry for life. It made her more vital to me, and I knew I would go through a lot to have that always. I didn't care what she was.

"Why me?" I said. "I'm a stranger to you."

"You're very quaint, dear."

"All right. How can you trust me?"

"What is there to trust? You mean I should be afraid of you going to Victor with what you think? Or perhaps suggesting things to the police?" She turned on the seat, regarding me coolly. "That would be a laugh, Victor would very likely hit you over the head with an oxygen tank." She paused and a smile touched the corners of her lips. "Besides, if he didn't, I would."

"No hokum. This is serious."

She said nothing for a moment. Her eyes were steady and cool. "Listen," she said. "I'm going to be serious. I think we understand each other very well, Jack. I mean by that, I don't believe either of us have any illusions concerning morality. Am I right?"

"Let's say you're right."

"I am right, darling—so very right. Tell you something, now. I did want the TV sets, and the speakers, the intercom units, for the house. But I'm not going to lie. I wanted the other, too." She leaned slightly toward me and there was a shade of bitterness in her tone. "I've been through hell with that man, taking care of him—I won't go into that now. It's too damned sordid. Suffice to say the past few years have been a prison for me. I've had very few acquaintances, none of the kind I've wanted, let alone anyone I could call a friend. I've been lonely. I don't have time for anything but taking care of him." Her voice tensed. "Alone all the time, like that, you get to doing things, thinking things, and sometimes you actually believe you'll go crazy."

"I can understand that."

"Yes. Can you understand this? I like to lie on my back with a man on top of me."

"I sort of guessed that the other day."

She showed me her teeth, gleaming and white and

maybe even predatory, between the red lips. Sometimes the things she said seemed to come from movies
she might have seen, or novels she might have read.
But it didn't matter. She said, "That's one of the
things I like about you. We're a pair, Jack. It's hot and
it will stay hot." She hesitated, then said, "So I wanted
the TV sets, but I counted on the other, too. I planned
for it. I thought of a lot of ways, and it seemed the
best. Lots of things could always go wrong with the
TV sets, or other things I'd buy. I didn't give a damn
who it was. A man, that's all, see?" Her face wasn't
pretty when she said that. You didn't want it pretty,
either. She breathed shallowly, her eyes clear and
young and bright. "If it didn't look as if it would work
out right, then I'd try another place, until I found
what I wanted. I didn't imagine it would be too
difficult, if I made things obvious. Only you were
different. I would have waited a long time."

"Oh, sure."

Her voice was low and tight. "You looked me over
and liked what you saw, and you thought about it. You
listened to every word I said, and thought about that.
You considered every angle till I thought I'd go crazy.
Like how old I was, and everything." She gave me
that sly look along her eyes. "I told you all about
Victor, so you'd know how it was with me. His having
an attack when he did was timed just right. You think
I needed your help, taking care of him? I could do
that in my sleep. But I knew you'd be sure then that I

did have it tough, and maybe I'd like to play around."

"You're really nuts, you know that?" She awed me. "You and Victor both should be in the hospital. You belong there."

"You laugh at me," she said, "and I'll dig your eyes out. I'm telling you, so you'll know."

"Okay."

Her voice softened. "I knew what you were thinking. There's only one thing, Jack. Now I don't want anybody else—ever. I just want you."

"Sure."

"I'm in love with you, Jack."

We sat there like that, watching each other.

Something coarse came into her tone. "I mean all I said. And don't try to kid me—you're as bad as I am."

"How do you mean, bad?"

She ran the tip of her tongue across her lips until they gleamed, and the excitement was in her eyes. "The other part of it," she said. "Victor. You were right. I thought all the things you said." She gave a quick sigh, straightened in the seat, and began looking at the windshield again. "But I could never do anything like that. I think about it—but it's just dreaming."

"The snow's getting pretty heavy now, Shirley. You'll have us drifted in if you don't watch it."

She slowly turned and frowned at me. "Just what do you mean?"

"I mean you're going to do it, Shirley. Someday you'd have to do it, you couldn't help yourself. So it's going to be now."

She stared at me, still frowning. She didn't speak.

"We're going to do it together," I said. "You know that."

Her lips moved very slightly, and there was no expression on her face at all.

"You mean you would help me?" she said.

"Yes."

The word hung there between us.

She slid across the seat and knelt on one knee, and put her arms around my neck, and pressed her mouth against mine. She shivered in my arms. I held her that way, then let go, and she slid back on the seat. Dim fright lurked in her eyes.

"I didn't know what you would say," she said. "I couldn't be absolutely sure."

"How do you feel now?"

"Good—crazy good."

She was wearing a fawn-colored dress of some slippery material that clung to her shape. Her eyes were very bright now, almost like glass. Her hair was thick and soft and full of light. The hem of the dress had worked far up on her thighs, past the rims of sheer, gartered stockings, twisted into the plump milk-white flesh.

I reached for her. She gave a little gasp and arched her back against the pressure of my hands, her breasts filling with the way she breathed as I pulled her up to me.

"You were here early," she said.

"So were you."

And then were locked together, and the car was shuddering in a storm of lust.

Much later we sat far apart and talked. Or Shirley talked.

"Mother was only married to Victor a year and a half before she died. Sometimes, when he's very ill, he gets the two of us mixed up. He thinks I'm his wife. But, anyway, everything comes to me when he dies. One thing that's worried me is the way he gives money away."

"How?"

"Don't get in a stew. There's plenty left." She reached over and patted my lips with her fingers, smiling. Then she got serious again. "Maybe there's more left now than he figures on giving me, even. He sold out for a frightful sum. But he makes these damned donations, it's like a disease. He gives to charities. It really scares me."

"For three years you've lived with this?"

She nodded. "Plus the year and a half before mother died. When she died, he just seemed to fall apart. Mother was his secretary for a while."

"He likes you a lot."

"He had nobody. I had nobody. It was one of those things." She smiled from the corners of her eyes. "I always sort of worked on him a little. It looked good to me."

"I can imagine. How much you figure he has right now? I mean cash in the bank?"

"Three—maybe four hundred thousand. I don't know exactly. About that."

"About—" I started to say something else, then stopped. I just sat there. It was my turn to stare at the windshield. It came to me how much money that was. I actually got a chill. In the back of my head, I'd had something like fifty, seventy-five thousand, and a split was there, too—twenty-five, maybe thirty for me. I hadn't brought it out clearly; it was just in the back of my head. But four hundred thousand dollars. She had said it as if it were three or four dollars.

I looked at her. She was watching me. The front or her dress was still undone. One full breast was bared, shaped like a honeydew melon, and her hair was snarled, the lipstick smeared. Her dress was rucked up in her lap, and her black nylon pants were hanging on the wind-wing handle. She looked hot enough to catch fire, but too lazy to do anything but just lie there and smoke.

The look of her, the smooth white flesh, stirred it all up in me again. I reached for her and kissed the nipple of her breast and then her mouth, and her fingers bit into my shoulders, the nails digging. She thrust herself away. "Not here—not again—somebody might—"

I couldn't let go of her.

Then she said, "I don't give a damn," and locked her arms around my neck. The instant she spoke, I did give a damn. If we were seen together from now on, out like this, the whole thing would have to be called off.

I let go of her, reached over and took her pants off the wind-wing handle and dropped them in her lap.

"Put 'em on," I said. "We're as nutty as they come. We've got to separate and get out of here." I told her why.

She lay back, pouting, and looking about sixteen. "I guess you're right," she said.

I offered her a cigarette, but she didn't want one. I lit up, waiting, trying to calm down. She got dressed, covered up, took a comb out of a small purse and began running it through her hair.

"Could he possibly be suspicious of you in any way?" I said. "Any way at all?"

"No." Her voice was flat now. "He even talks of how he'll live another twenty years. How I'll always be at his side. Like that."

"Shirley," I said. "We can't wait on this. We've got to pull it off as soon as possible."

"When?"

"Soon. I'll think about it." It was as if we were discussing a get-together between friends. I said, "Listen, didn't he ever want you to go to school?"

"I went to private schools," she said. "But when

mother died, he wanted me to stay with him." She paused. "Jack," she said, turning in the seat, looking at me as she combed the snarls out of her hair. "You can't begin to imagine what this has done to me. Being with him every hour of the day, the way he is. Seeing him live on and on. Watching months and years go down the drain. Knowing they'll try to get him into a hospital eventually, maybe any day." She quit combing and her eyes got that glazed, absent look. "Knowing that even if I manage to keep him out of a hospital, it'll be bedpans and dirty sheets and giving him baths and all the rest of that stinking that goes with it." She stared at the windshield and put her hand over her mouth, then took it away. "You can't imagine. Nobody can."

"I can. Rugged."

"He won't die. He just won't die. He's not really supposed to get out of bed, except when he has to— and God believe me, I would make him crawl on his hands and knees."

"No," I said. "You wouldn't. You'd fetch the bedpan, and do your job, because all he'd have to do is complain just once to this Miraglia—even joking—and that would be that. He'd have a registered nurse in there so fast you'd hardly know it happened."

"Don't frighten me. But you're right. Doctor Miraglia says he can stay up a little. Victor wants to be up a lot. I let him. It's our secret. I try to even urge him, carefully, of course, thinking something might happen."

"You ever think maybe it makes him stronger?"

"I'm trapped," she said. "I'll go out of my mind."

"Not now. Remember?"

She said, "This doesn't seem wrong at all, Jack." She lowered her voice. "I've come to hate him—hate everything about him. He's stealing my life. He's taken my fun, and I can't escape because of that damned money he holds over my head. He doesn't talk about it. It's just there, in his eyes, in the way he grins at me. I don't even think of him as a person any more."

"Easy, now. I understand."

"You can't really understand, Jack. Not really. Nobody could." It was there in her eyes. "He's like a corpse, only he can't be decently buried."

"I get you."

"And you don't even know him. He's nothing to you, so it shouldn't really matter to you, either."

"It doesn't matter."

Her eyes got dreamy. "To be free. God, to be free again. Free to come and go. Free—to have you, Jack— free to breathe again, without hate."

"You're getting poetic."

She laughed softly. Her eyes were misty. "I guess— I guess I just can't help it."

"You weren't thinking of anything like dropping that TV set on his face, were you?"

"I read it in a magazine. Somebody had a TV set on his ceiling, so he could watch it, lying in bed. I kept thinking about it. I couldn't forget it."

"You'd have lasted about ten minutes after the cops got there. They'd have torn you apart. Listen, Shirley—I am going to put that TV set up there on the ceiling. But it'll be up so damned solid you won't get it down without pulling the roof with it."

"What, then?"

"It's obvious. No air."

The corners of her mouth tipped up. "You think that hasn't occurred to me about a thousand times?" Her eyes lidded faintly. "Every time I hold that mask over his face I have to fight myself to turn on the oxygen."

"That's right," I said. "You turn it on—only you just don't put the mask over his face."

"I don't agree with you."

"That's how it's got to be."

She didn't say anything.

"Only it won't be quite that simple," I said. "There'll be more to it." I reached across her and opened the door. "I've got half an idea. I want to work on it. You run along. I'll meet you at your place, with the truck, and take up where I left off. I won't come till the doc's gone."

She put her hand to her mouth. "I forgot. I'd better hurry." She got out. "I told Victor you were busy with something unavoidable that came up. I told him you'd be back."

"Pretty sure of yourself."

"I prayed you would."

She went to her car. Well, so far Victor was just an

old half-dead bastard who was going to finish dying. I had to keep it that way. The minute conscience stepped in, you were in trouble.

She drove off, and I sat there, and she was no more than out of hearing when I began to worry. One slip-up was all we needed. I'd forgotten to tell her to prepare a sound alibi for where she'd been.

I gunned the car out of there and went tearing down the boulevard. It was too late. She was gone.

I pulled over to the curb and stopped the car, and sat there gripping the steering wheel, knowing I would go through with this thing. All my life I'd been waiting for a chance like this. Keep your eyes and ears open and stay tuned in, and one day there it is. If you don't want it, you don't have to touch it. And it's not half frightening, or anything like that. Shirley and I generated something together that drowned out conscience. This was just something we were going to do together. And, of course, the money. I wanted it. I would get it. All I had to do was make him die in a way that looked natural, and make the whole thing look legitimate. And there would be Shirley, too.

Thinking that made it better still. Shirley Angela was under my skin like the itch and it was going to take a lot of scratching.

He was ready to die. He was old enough. He sure as hell was rich enough.

Then I thought, "But you never killed."

So there had to be a first time. It wouldn't be hard. It would just barely be killing, if you looked at it right. And there would be no more Grace; something that had gone on too long already with no way to top her.

We were going to kill Victor Spondell for his money, and that's how it was going to be.

I went downstairs and had Veronica Lewis, a babe I knew, run a quick check on Victor Spondell's bankroll. It would be okay, because I was doing a big job for him. Everything Shirley Angela had said was true. I didn't get the exact figure, but I wasn't worried if it came to a split.

Five

It wasn't dark yet. We were in the back yard, and she was helping me figure placement for a couple of speakers out there. I carried a folding ruler, and kept measuring tree trunks and the side of the house, craning my neck around to make it look good, in case anybody happened to see us.

I said, "You can't stay out here long. You better keep running back into the house, so you can check on him. Isn't that what you'd do normally?"

"Yes."

"Did the doctor have anything to say when you got back?"

"He told me Victor should be in the hospital."

I chewed the inside of my cheek.

She said, "He didn't speak to Victor about it, though. Because it riles him up. I told them I'd been shopping. I stopped on the way home and bought a lot of stuff; I just grabbed everything in sight."

"Good. But we can't be seen together again, away from this place—not once."

"All right."

"You do everything just as you'd normally do it," I said. "Try to imagine me as exactly what I am—a TV serviceman, who's installing two television sets and an intercom system in your home. Try and remember that."

"All right, Jack."

"One thing we've got to be absolutely certain of. If he has one of his attacks, will he positively die if he doesn't get oxygen?"

She stared at me. She didn't speak.

"What's the matter?" I said.

"It just struck me for a minute—what we're doing."

"Listen," I said. "You go soft on this and it's all off. Got that? If either one of us goes soft, we've got to quit."

She nodded. "I'll be all right."

"See that you are. Make damned sure."

"I'm sure."

"Okay. Would he die if he didn't get oxygen?"

"Yes. It might take a little time, but he'll die. He'll suffocate, choke to death. Excitement hastens it. Then when he can't get air, he gets scared. If nobody helps him, he'll choke to death. That is, if his heart doesn't go first."

"He's in a hell of a shape, isn't he."

She didn't say anything. I went to the rear of the house, brought back a ladder, and leaned it against the pine tree. I climbed up three rungs and made it look as if I were inspecting the tree trunk.

I said, "Does the doc give him anything to keep his nerves steady?"

"Yes. He takes nerve pills regularly. And he takes

some other stuff to help prevent the forming of mucous. He takes nitroglycerin pills for his heart pains, and the doctor gives him shots to help dehydrate him, so liquid won't form."

"God. Why does he want to live, anyway?"

"He has spells when he's quite well," she said. "He feels good. He thinks eventually all of this will pass and he'll feel fine again. He was always an energetic man. He won't believe he's done for."

"How often do these attacks occur?"

"You never know. He's gone as long as three months without any trouble at all. Excitement helps bring them on."

I hadn't figured on waiting any length of time like that. Get it over with was my idea. Waiting that long, I would be in as bad shape as she was.

"But," she said, "sometimes he's had as many as four attacks in one week. And the intervals are getting shorter. That's why all the talk about getting him to a hospital, where they could put him in an oxygen tent and administer to him better.'

I came down the ladder, picked the ladder up, and carried it over to a coconut palm by the seawall. I was perspiring and it wasn't from carrying the ladder. She tagged along.

"You better run in and make a check," I said. "Come back as soon as you can."

"How are we going to do it, Jack?"

"I want your ideas, first." I cleared my throat.

"Shirley—it'll never happen—but suppose after it's done, we get split up somehow. Say, if we have to. Do I have your word we'll divide the money?"

"You have my word." Her lips were a little tense. She turned and headed for the house. I'd had to say that. I watched the way she stuck out in back, with high heels on. She still wore the fawn-colored dress. That walk of hers could drive a man nuts.

I put the ladder against the palm, stared at the Gulf, and lit a cigarette. Then I started up the ladder with the ruler, and it hit me how we would do this thing.

I stood there hanging to the ladder. It was going to be taking one hell of a sweet chance. A single slip, the measliest mistake, the wiggle of an eyebrow at the wrong time, and I was personally as good as strapped into the frying chair.

My palms were wet. But there it was. The one way. The right way. I still wanted to hear what she might have to say, but I knew beforehand that nothing she could ever come up with would be as simple and clear-cut and perfect as what had struck me.

I stood there in a land of trance, till I'd gone over every angle, and the hot coal of the cigarette began to burn my lips. I spat it out.

"Mr. Ruxton?"

I hadn't heard her come across the lawn. I wondered why in hell she was calling me "Mr. Ruxton," and turned on the ladder. She stood there, smiling up at me. A medium-sized guy carrying a small black bag stood beside her.

"Mr. Ruxton," she said. "This is Doctor Miraglia, Mr. Spondell's doctor. I told him what I was having done, and he thinks it's an excellent idea."

I came down the ladder, taking long quiet breaths, trying to get a good look at him. He had a polite little smile and a clean, well-scrubbed look. He wore gray slacks and a white shirt. His face was round and earnest looking, and rimless glasses rode a little low on a pug nose. He had thick black hair. He was maybe forty. I shook his hand.

He nodded in a very polite way and said, "I believe this is a fine idea Shirley has, Mr. Ruxton. It hadn't occurred to me. But since our tough old boy won't go to a hospital, this will give Shirley a little more freedom around the place."

"It should make things easier," I said.

He looked up at the coconut palm, just to be looking someplace, then at me again, very polite. Then he turned and smiled briefly at Shirley. "I'll be very interested to see how it works when it's finished," he said. His voice was mild and easygoing, gentle. He probably had a great way with the bed-patients. He looked at me, the glasses glinting a little. "Reason I wanted to meet you," he said, "I wanted to say, be gentle with the old boy when you explain about this intercom system and how it works. He'll probably get rambunctious, and try to order you around, and he won't want to listen. Be gentle but stern—and make sure he knows how to operate it."

"Sure," I said. "Don't you worry."

"There won't be any trouble, Doctor," she said.

"Well," he said. "I've got to run. Glad to have met you, Mr. Ruxton. If I have any trouble with our television, I'll know who to call."

"Any time. Twenty-four hour service." I felt like a blabbermouth fool, saying that, and looked at her to see how she was doing. She was doing fine.

"He's a rough old bird," Miraglia said.

I didn't speak. He nodded again, glanced at her, and they turned and walked along toward the front of the house. He was explaining something to her. She kept nodding, but I saw the stiffness of her shoulders and knew his being here had worried her.

In a few minutes she was back. "There was nothing I could do," she said. "He showed up and I never knew he was coming back. Said he was passing by the house, so he decided to drop off a fresh supply of medicine. Then I had to tell him about you being here, and he wanted to meet you."

"It's okay," I said. "It's perfect. Just keep acting natural. Think like I told you. Everything on the up and up." Some of the tightness went away from around her eyes. She relaxed and gave a little sigh. "Jack," she said, "I've just got to know how we're going to do this. It keeps hanging over my head."

"What ideas you got?"

She lowered her voice. It was coming into mid-twilight now, and she looked terrific. The sun had turned into reds and purples out there over the Gulf, with long shooting lines of crimson, like wild fire up across the skies. Some of the colors got into her hair, and played along her body, accentuating the curves. I wanted to take her in my arms, and just hold her and feel the way she'd stir against me. I wanted her bad again. It was primitive and hot. Her lips were parted a little and I knew how they would be.

She said, "I can read you like a book."

"Start wearing a barrel, then."

"Maybe I'd better." She moved her hip a little, and it was worse than before.

"Cut it out," I said. "I'll throw you on the ground."

"Wish you would."

I took hold of the ladder, looking up at the palm tree.

She said, "If you say the TV set on the ceiling is out, then all right. I just don't go for this 'no air' idea of yours. I was thinking maybe he could take a bad fall. Something not so obvious."

"It's got to be obvious. That's the angle."

"But don't you see? I mean—unless I broke a leg and couldn't get to him, how would it work? It's my job to watch him, Jack—all the time."

"Yeah."

"Unless we bolixed up the oxygen tanks, somehow. Maybe that would be good."

I shook my head. "You wouldn't last a minute. And I'm damned if you're going to break one of those legs."

"All right, Einstein—how, then?"

I said, "Walk toward the house. I'll carry the ladder. I want to put a speaker on the side of the house, anyway—so I can check there. Now, listen. It's going to be perfect."

"It's got to be perfect."

"Yeah. First of all, there's going to be a patsy— somebody with the blame on him. That's the best way, see? Because then they won't look any further. If they know how it happened and who actually caused it, then it's all over. Right?"

"I don't believe I understand, Jack."

"The blame's going to be on me," I said. "It's as simple as that."

She stopped walking. "On you?"

We had reached the house. I stuck the ladder up and crawled up two rungs, speaking low. "I'm not taking any real chance. Unless something goes wrong. And I don't see how anything can go wrong. It's going to be obvious you've done everything you can for Victor. You're fixing him up with television, and the house is wired so you can hear him calling no matter where you are. So what's the obvious thing?"

She stared up at me. "I can't hear him?"

"Right." I came down by her again. "You don't hear him. He's calling weakly. I heard him call, remember. It's faint. If you're not damned close by, you'll miss it. Out here, for example. So that's how come the intercom, and he's using the intercom. As far as anybody's concerned, you never heard a thing. You can be standing there looking at him, for all it matters. We'll work that out. But it's going to be that clean."

"I don't understand at all, Jack,"

"I'm going to fix that unit by his bed so it goes on the blink. And it'll be my fault."

"But they'll find it."

"Certainly they'll find it. But it'll be fixed in such a way that it won't be on purpose. See? Just plain carelessness on my part. A mistake. They can't hang you for making a fool mistake, can they? Sure, they'll raise hell, and you'll raise hell, and there'll be talk, but so what? He'll be dead. Don't worry, I can do it."

"How?"

"First of all. I'll put the units in, and we'll let them go for a couple of days so he can wear the newness out of it, get used to it. He'll be using it all the time, calling you, talking to you. It's always that way when people first get them in their homes. Then it'll die off. You can maybe work in a word to him, ask him to use it only if he has to. Like if he has an attack. He won't mind, after he's played with it for a while."

"Will you please tell me how you'll work it? It sounds complicated."

"It's perfect. Look, it's going to be careless soldering. A condenser's going to go bad and I'll have to put a new one in."

"What's a condenser?"

"Never mind. The point is this. It's a coupling condenser, and it'll be soldered to the grid terminal of a tube socket. Now, when I solder it in I'm going to do a sloppy job. I'll know it's a sloppy job, but I'm in a hurry—I've got another call. So I try the intercom and it works. So I say to hell with it."

"If it works, what good is the idea?"

"Here's the idea. When the unit's turned on for any length of time, the metal on the grid will expand from the heat. It'll ground out. That means the unit won't function. It's that simple."

"But if he calls me, he isn't just going to sit there and wait for metal to expand."

"Shirley. It will only take a minute. And you're forgetting this is staged for them when they look around. They'll find him dead. You'll make absolutely sure he's dead before you do a thing. Like, if he uses the intercom to call you when he has an attack, and it works, you'll just have to hold off going in to him till he dies. The unit will go off. It could go off the minute he turns the thing on."

"Suppose it doesn't go off?"

"But it will, Shirley."

"Suppose he just uses it to call me. Maybe he just wants me to bring him something. I mean, before he has an attack, and it goes off? What then?"

"I thought of that, too. You just stick within hearing distance, like you do now, until the time comes when you know he's having an attack. He'll never know whether the unit's working or not. See? There's nothing can go wrong. Just the same, I'll go over every point a hundred times, before we pull it."

"I'm beginning to see. It's good, Jack—it's good."

"Sure. So they find him dead. The intercom's turned on. Obviously he was trying to call you. Only you were out here, sitting by the Gulf, and you didn't hear a thing. You're all broken up. The unit's inspected. They find what? They find I did a careless soldering job. The set grounded out. He was trying to get you, but the unit wasn't working. It's my fault. I'm to blame. But did I actually kill him? Nobody'll ever go so far as to say I did. It's a human error."

"Isn't that taking an awful chance?"

"Sure. But you think of a better way, and tell me about it. Don't you see? I'll be sick about it, I'll feel like hell. But what can I do? Resurrect him?"

"Jack—it's really good."

"Sure." I motioned with my head. "We'd better get inside. It's getting dark, and I'd better take off. It'll look better if I come around in the morning, work in the daytime. We can iron out any snarls then. You try to think of flaws, all night, and I'll do the same. Try to think of anything that could go wrong."

"All right."

We moved around the side of the house. "I wish you could stay," she said.

"I can't. We've got to take it real easy."

We walked up the ramp onto the front porch. The front screen door opened, and a woman stepped out on the porch. She was very thin, with long blonde hair, and she was wearing a pair of dungarees and a loose white blouse. She looked the nervous type, and loud.

"Shirley," she said. Her voice was raspy, like the edge of a tin can against slate, "Where've you been, honey? I've looked all over hell for you."

This was great.

"Mayda," Shirley said. "What is it?"

The woman looked at me and made with the sideward glance, waggling penciled eyebrows.

"I'd like to borrow handsome, here. For just a few minutes," she said. She was maybe thirty-two or three. "I thought you were inside, so I just crashed the gate. You know me."

Shirley gave me a quick helpless look and tried to tell me something with her eyes that I couldn't get.

"Mr. Ruxton," Shirley said. "This is my next door neighbor, Mayda Lamphier."

"Free, white and twenty-one," the woman said. She waggled her eyebrows again. "What I mean is, my husband's in Alaska. He won't be back for six months. You can imagine how that is, can't you?"

"What's up?" Shirley said.

"He's a TV fixer-upper, isn't he?"

I said, "Yes."

"Well, daddy," she said to me. "My set's acting up.

I saw your truck over here." She regarded Shirley with a smile. "I figured maybe I could borrow him for a few minutes. It's probably nothing more than some adjustment." She gave with the eyebrows again. "The set, of course, honey."

"I'm just leaving," I said. "Be glad to take a look." I turned to Shirley. "See you in the morning, Miss Angela. I'll try to get everything installed as quickly as possible."

"Thanks, Mr. Ruxton."

This was something Shirley hadn't warned me about. It troubled her. I felt bad about it.

We went across to Mayda's house and tinkered with the set.

"You were right," I said to Mayda Lamphier. "It was just the horizontal hold out of kilter. You could've fixed it yourself."

"But it's so much nicer having you do it. What do I owe you?"

"Nothing. Glad to help."

"How's for one for the road?"

"One what?"

"Oh, come, darling. Give me time to get my breath." She gushed some laughter, eyeing me, and meaning damned well everything she said. "A drink is what I meant."

"Thanks just the same. I've got to get back."

"I'm all alone in this house," she said. "I've been

married for ten years. This is the first time my husband's ever been away. Think of that."

I thought of that.

"Know what I mean?" she said.

"You sure must miss him."

"I don't miss him worth a hang." she said. "You know what I mean."

I looked over at her TV set, in the dimly lighted room. "If you'll just leave that the way it is, it'll probably stay okay for a long while."

"You won't hang around?"

"I'm sorry. The business keeps me hopping."

"How you like Shirl?"

"Miss Angela, you mean?"

"You know who I mean, honey."

"She seems like a nice kid," I said. I turned and started over toward the door.

"She's sure tied down with that old monkey," Mayda Lamphier said. "Know what I mean?"

I opened the front door, turned and looked at her.

She waggled her eyebrows, smiling. "You're real cute," she said. "Maybe Shirl won't have to go running off so much, with you around."

I hung onto the door. "I don't get you," I said quizzically.

"Come, now, darling. She's always running downtown, running off. Stuck with that old geezer, and as young as she is. I don't blame her. She's missing out on all the fun, and she knows it. At her age, she should be having boyfriends—but she doesn't have a one. I mean, not that you can see. I don't blame her, whatever she does. Not really."

Not much, she didn't. This one was a knife with a sharp blade. Just the same, it was good, having met her. I figured I had acted right with her.

"Well," I said. "That's how it goes."

"You'll be around—over at Shirl's?"

"Some work I have to do. It might take a couple of days."

"I might need you again."

"Okay. So long."

I walked out into the street and around the hedge, and back to where I had left the truck parked in the driveway. Shirley was in the shadow of the porch, standing in the driveway.

"Make it look right," I said, as I came up to the truck. "She's got a nose forty feet long, and eyes like telescopes. She's got to be stopped from going in your house. I don't care how you do it. But do it. Tell her the doctor said nobody's to come in, because of Victor. Got that?"

"All right, Mr. Ruxton," she said, just loud enough so it would carry across the hedge. Then she got a little closer to me and spoke softly. "I was going to tell you about her. She's perfectly harmless. She just thinks she's full of hell."

"Thinks or is," I said. "Stop her. Coral snakes are

harmless, too—if you stay away from them. It's okay for now, because she really believes everything's on the up and up. We've got to keep it that way. Get back inside, and I'll see you tomorrow."

"Oh, God, Jack—if you could only stay." I started the truck up and backed out into the street. Mayda Lamphier was walking back and forth in her living room. I saw her through the windows.

Six

I didn't sleep worth a damn that night. I smoked cigarettes and lay there staring up at the ceiling, thinking about everything. I went over every detail, and I didn't see how it could miss.

I got so excited my heart acted as if it had started freewheeling. It wouldn't slow down. My breathing was all cockeyed, and I couldn't lie still in the bed. I tried lying every way possible. Nothing worked. I held my breath, trying to slow down my heart and it would slow down, but the second I started breathing again it began hammering. Through it all I kept trying not to think of her, because she stirred me up so bad, just thinking of her, I knew I'd never sleep. I'd be lying there talking to her in my mind, laughing a little to myself, and once I caught myself motioning with my hands, explaining to her how everything would run smooth, and how we'd have the money, and then I'd be kissing her, with my hands snarled in her hair, and we'd be wild. So I'd get up.

I tried fixing a stiff drink. It only made things worse. So I quit trying to sleep. I took a scratch pad, and pencil, and got in bed, and lay there figuring loopholes. I made lists of everything I could think of. I put her down in black and white. *Shirley Angela*. I tried to coldly analyze all the movements she would make from the time *Victor* had *The Attack* until after the will was probated, and we had the money, and then the waiting after that. I'd find myself lying back staring into a misty pastel *Rio de Janeiro,* with her laughing and pushing against me with her hip, or maybe the two of us lying in a ritzy hotel bedroom on one of those oversized beds. And she would be naked, with that auburn hair fanned out around her head on the pillow.

So then I began all over again, with the intercom units. I would solder the coupling condenser to the grid terminal, and do a sloppy job.

I thought about how I would act, how sorry I would be when they told me it was my fault he died. So I got off that tack, right away, and began thinking about the big beds with her again, and somewhere along in there I konked off and Shirley Angela turned into Mayda Lamphier. I kept chasing Mayda Lamphier through an endless living room full of TV sets. She would stand on a TV set, and take off pieces of clothing, until she was leaping from one TV set to the other with nothing on but a raggedy blouse, flapping out behind her. I caught her. Just as I got my hands on her, she gave a yell, and this Doctor Miraglia popped up from behind all the TV sets. I came awake in a sweat.

I got up and burned all the paper I'd been figuring on, and flushed it down the john. It was daylight outside.

The buzzer sounded. It was Grace at the door.

"I just stopped over to say goodbye," she said.

"Okay," I said. "Goodbye." I started to close the door.

"Goddamn you, Jack!"

She lunged against the door and came into the apartment. She stood there looking at me. I wasn't sure whether she would cry or scream or what.

"I told you not to come here," I said. "For Christ's sake, it's practically still dark outside."

She began pacing up and down, rubbing her hands together. I watched her. I didn't like any part of it. All I wanted to do was get her the hell out of here. She was slim and blonde, with a tightly packed, well-shaped body. She had on a fresh pink dress, and she wasn't carrying anything, not even a purse. She always walked kind of heavy on her heels, and I watched her breasts jiggle as she moved around the room. She was trying to look determined, and having a hard time of it.

"What do you want?" I said. "Look, Grace. Start using your head, will you?"

She turned and stared at me for maybe three seconds, her eyes real cool. "All right, Jack. I wanted this to go right. I see it hasn't. It never will. I'm going away, leaving town. I'll quit bothering you. I wanted to say I'm sorry." She started pounding toward the door, and stopped in front of me, and her lips twisted with it. "But I'm not sorry."

"Okay. So long, Grace. Take care of yourself, for old times' sake."

She was a finagling woman. Sometimes she more than just scared me. I stood there waiting for her to go, afraid to say anything else for fear she'd take it wrong. No matter what you said, Grace would take it as an insult, or some kind of probe among her defenses.

"You won't see me again," she said. "Don't worry."

I still didn't say anything. I wondered if she was going to start the suicide bit again. She didn't. She kept looking at me for a minute, with her mouth kind of twisted up that way, then she went over to the door, and out into the hall. She slammed the door. I listened to her walking away down the hall, the heels smacking.

The next day was rough. I worked hard and got the intercom units wired into the house. I left the business about the television set on the ceiling in his bedroom until last, because I figured to get the intercoms in so he could fiddle with them and get tired of them as soon as possible.

We had a few minutes in the kitchen when I first started working; we went over everything together again. She had come up with one or two minor snags, like Doctor Miraglia showing right at the moment when Victor was dying, or Victor maybe somehow getting out of bed and running into the street because she wasn't helping him. I told her those were chances we had to take. I convinced her they wouldn't happen.

"I spoke to Mayda," she said. "I told her Victor had to have absolute quiet from now on, and he mustn't get excited, so she shouldn't come into the house. I told her I was very sorry. She understood, all right."

"She's a big mouth," I said. "She might mention it to Miraglia, later on, and he'd say he never gave any such orders."

"I'll tell him about her, when I see him. I'll tell him I used him as an excuse to get rid of her because she's such a bore."

"Good. That's perfect."

"She mentioned you."

"Yeah."

"It's all right, though. I fixed that. I told her you were an awful dope, stuff like that. How you couldn't wait to finish the job. I didn't make any big thing of it, of course."

"Shirley," I said. "I just thought of something. You'll have to impress this on your mind until it's an automatic action. The speakers I'm going to put up out back in the yard will have a volume control. You'll have to see that they're turned off. And as soon as he's—gone, you'll have to turn them on—and you can't be seen doing it. It would cook us. If he started yelling over the intercom before the unit grounds out, somebody would sure as hell hear him."

"Could they hear him from inside the house?"

"His voice is too weak to carry that far. Like as not, the unit will short right out. Now, don't worry about that. I can do it perfect. But you've got to be sure you turn those speakers on, because that's where you'll say you were when it happened. In the dark, by the Gulf, sitting. You can say you like to sit out there at night."

"I'll remember. You'll have to show me the volume controls."

"Yeah."

"Jack, you don't think they'll suspect us."

"How can they? Don't you worry. It'll be my fault, like I said, and that won't mean a thing. I'm just a television repairman, see? There's nothing between you and me. We've only just met. That's the first thing. Any number of people can attest to that. They'll never suspect you. All they'll think is that you got a break." I hesitated, and pulled her to me, and kissed her, then let her go, because I didn't want anything starting up right then. "Know what the word will be?" I said. "They'll say, Poor old Spondell, he's better off dead. He was suffering. It's a shame to say it, but you're better off, and he's better off. All these years you've nursed him, waited on him hand and foot. If they think anything bad, it'll be counteracted by their own thoughts that he's better off dead."

"Don't say it anymore, Jack."

"I know. It kind of gets you, sometimes. But, listen, Shirley. We can't be seen together, and you can't call me. I'll contact you somehow, if need be. We can use the alibi of my coming out here to adjust something—once, maybe twice. No more. I'll be out once to solder the condenser. We should leave it at that."

"I'll go crazy."

"No, you won't."

It wasn't easy, the way she paraded around the rest of the day. She had on a pair of white shorts and a white sweater. The only thing that kept me from busting a seam was the thought of what we'd have when it was all over.

I explained to Victor how the unit in his room worked. He got a kick out of it. He was like a kid.

"All you have to do is flip that switch, and talk," I told him. "Simple."

"Maybe you're not such a son of a bitch, after all, Ruxton," he said, grinning up at me. There were little dabs of bright red coloring on his cheeks today, and his eyes were bright. He looked over where she was standing at the foot of the bed, by those feet. "Shirley," he said. "Honey, you go out in the kitchen and listen for me. Say something."

She did. It went on that way. He kept her jumping and pretty well tied up, talking nonsense from one room to the other, playing radio announcer, and imitating Jack Benny.

Like a kid, he was.

Just the same, he was going to die.

All the time I worked, I kept going over and over

every point on the program. I examined each point from all angles. It occurred to me that Victor would want to show Miraglia how the intercoms worked. Shirley would have to go along with that and show some excitement. I told her, and she okayed it.

While I was out back putting up the two PA speakers, one on the coconut palm and the other on the side of the house, somebody called.

"Hello, handsome."

It was Mayda Lamphier, over in her yard, beyond the hedge. I nodded and kept working. She stood there for a while, wanting to say something. She gave it up, and went inside her house.

I put the speakers down just low enough so Shirley could reach the volume controls.

We had to move his bed so I could fasten the TV set on the ceiling. I worked with a ladder, with him lying in bed, watching. I got the set up there with a sling hoist, and bolted it to brackets fastened through the ceiling to rafters.

Shirley kept saying, "Are you all right, Mr. Ruxton? Can I help you, Mr. Ruxton?"

I just grunted.

When I finished, I was knocked out, but it was up there to stay. You could chin yourself on it, if you wanted, it was that solid. There was a fair picture even without the antenna, so we rolled his bed over into place and let him watch some local hillbilly program. He seemed happy.

Outside, she held the ladder while I headed for the roof with the antenna.

"He can have two days to play around," I said. "Will the doctor be here by then?"

"He comes tomorrow."

"Good; then Victor can put on an exhibition with the intercoms and get that out of his system. He can have tomorrow and the next day—then I'm coming to fix the condenser."

"How will I make him think something's wrong?"

"I'll show you," I told her. "You'll pull the main light switch, and knock everything out."

She didn't say anything. I looked at her and got that feeling. She was staring at me, with her eyes hot, her teeth tight together, and her lips parted a little.

She spoke softly. "I want to see you, Jack."

"Yeah."

"What will we do?"

"I don't know."

It was hell, what she did to me. She was right there, asking for it. And I could have her, only I couldn't have her. She pushed against the edge of the ladder and said, "Jesus, Jack. What will we do?"

"We'll have to wait," I said. "You'll have to be here when the doctor comes tomorrow. I want to know everything they do and say."

"All right. But, I can't wait, Jack. I'm burning up."

"We've got to wait. You think it's easy for me?"

She just watched me. Her look really got me. I

went up the ladder fast, and put up the antenna, a
double V, and fixed the lead. Then I came down and
went in to see how Victor was making out.

"He's sleeping," she said. "He always naps along
about now. He'll sleep for at least fifteen minutes."

Her eyes were foggy.

"Where's the fuse box? There's time to show you."

I followed her out through the kitchen, watching
the way she moved under those tight white shorts.
The fuse box was in a utility room off the back of the
house. There was a lot of junk in the room; a wicker
clothes hamper, electric hot-water heater, washing
machine, some garden tools, and an electric lawn
mower. There was a big pile of clothes on the floor.

I showed her the switch and told her to pull it the
first thing in the morning, three days from now, and
then phone me at the store.

I turned on the light in the utility room, then
pulled the main switch, to show her how everything
went off. Then I turned the juice back on, and turned
off the light.

"Jack?"

The utility room door was partially closed. We were
in shadow. I turned when she spoke, hearing the way
she breathed. It was like being dragged fast through
a knot hole. She had peeled off those shorts and she
wanted to make sure I knew it.

I held her and she squirmed and panted. "I couldn't
wait, Jack. I couldn't wait!"

We fell down on the pile of clothes. Right then it started. All through the house, from every room. His voice. Calling. Echoing:

"Shirley? Hey, Honey. Oh, Shirl? Bring me a coke, will you? Hey, Shirley. Come on, Honey—calling all cars, come to the corner bedroom, Victor Spondell is in dire need of sustenance in the way of a cold Coca-Cola."

She crouched and began to curse him. I'd never heard anything like it. The language she used would have shamed a drunken Marine.

"Honey? Shirl? Where are you? Calling all cars. Disregard code signals. Go to the bedroom of...."

I got up and hauled her to her feet.

"You've got to go in there. Get a move on."

Her face was flushed, her mouth twitching.

"Hurry up," I said.

She yanked her shorts on.

"You wait right here," she said. "I'll be back!"

She went into the kitchen. I heard her speak to him over the intercom, sweet as syrup, and he came back with some of his bright wit. The refrigerator door slammed and shook the place. I heard her uncap a bottle of coke and pour it into a glass. Then she thundered through the house.

I waited. Nothing. Silence.

I waited a long time, sitting on the pile of clothes.

Finally I went through the house, and looked into

the bedroom. She was seated in a chair beside his bed, reading to him.

I said, "Sorry to interrupt. I guess everything's in order now."

She looked up at me. Her expression was as if somebody had shot her in the face with salt. "Victor wanted me to read to him," she said. She turned to him, smiling. "I'll have to pay Mr. Ruxton, now, Victor."

"All right," he said. He said to me, "Thanks for everything you've done, Ruxton. Sure appreciate it. Makes things a lot easier, eh?" He laughed and coughed a little.

She came out, fuming.

I said, "You'd better pay me, and I'll write out a receipt, just in case."

He had already written out a check, and she had cashed it at the bank, to cover the expense of the installations. She counted out the money in bills, from her purse.

"Wouldn't he arrange for a joint account?" I said.

She shook her head. "He never went for that. He won't let anybody take care of him but me. He could afford nurses around the clock, and live in the finest places. He wants it this way. But he writes the checks. Sometimes, when we've had little arguments, he's hinted how I may have it tough now, but I'll get mine, someday. I honestly think there's a mean streak in him—he gets enjoyment out of doing things the way he does."

We were in her bedroom. She was in bad shape.

I said, "Remember, after I fix that condenser, it's not going to be easy. The units will probably go out, and you'll have to stick close to his room, so it'll seem they're on. You won't be able to talk back to him—he wouldn't hear anything. It's a ticklish part, Shirley. If he catches on, before anything happens, you'll just have to call me and we'll go through the whole thing again."

"I couldn't stand it."

"Well, then I was thinking. If you can excite him, some way—help bring on an attack. Think you could swing it?"

"Yes. I've seen it happen."

I took hold of her shoulders. "That's what you'll have to do. We've got to work fast, once I do that soldering job."

"I wish he were dead. God, how I wish it."

"He will be."

There wasn't anything in the world now, but us. I held her close and tight and it all started up again. I had never wanted any woman the way I wanted Shirley Angela.

"Shirley?" His voice blared from the unit beside her bed. *"This is Car 77, calling Headquarters...."*

Seven

Waiting for her to call the store was a nightmare. Every time the phone rang, I had to grit my teeth to keep from jumping. I thought of a thousand things that could go wrong, but the big one was that she might lose her nerve.

Finally she called on the morning of the third day. I let Pete Stallsworth answer the phone, even though I was practically running standing still.

"Jack?" he said. "It's for you." He grinned, covered the mouthpiece, and whispered, "Sounds like real stuff. What a voice. Va-voom!"

"Okay." I was plenty nervous. I said, "Ruxton speaking."

"It's all set," she said. "I flipped the switch. And it's like you said, Jack. It doesn't bother him much that it's not working. He's over the excitement of it, and I've talked him into using it only for emergencies. I told him to remember, that was why we really had it installed. He's taken to watching TV, now."

"I see," I said, loud enough so Pete Stallsworth could hear. "I'll be right out. I'm very sorry you've had this inconvenience."

"He just says to have it fixed."

"All right."

"There's something I'd personally like fixed, too."

"What's that?"

"You guess."

She could be like a bomb, sometimes. I went out there, driving the truck like a madman. I had been practicing soldering connections and making a sloppy job of it, for two days. The right kind of perfect, sloppy job. I had it so pat I could make a unit ground out with my eyes closed, and time it to within a matter of seconds.

I parked in her drive, got out the tools, and went to the door. She opened the screen with her knee.

She whispered it. "I wore a skirt."

"Well, keep it down," I shot at her. "I want to be steady now."

She was lovely. I wanted to stand there and stare at her. Her eyes were full of excitement, and her hair was brushed out thick and full. She wore a white blouse with a big curling starched collar, and a full, fluffed out print skirt, loaded with splotches of color.

His bedroom door was closed.

"Jack," she said. "We almost fouled up."

"How do you mean?"

"When I turned off the main switch, the TV set went off, too."

It had completely slipped my mind. I broke out in a sweat.

"It's all right," she said. "I figured it out. I put the

switch back on when he mentioned it, then just loosened the fuse for his section of the house. It's marked on the box."

"Good girl," I said. "That was close."

From then on, I intended to be a lot more careful. It showed me how easy it was to miss on some point, even when you were watching everything. It was an obvious point. That's what made it so bad.

We went into his room. He lay there with his gray eyebrows snarling, and gave me the glad, "Hello, Ruxton. How's the old son-of-a-bitch, today?"

I didn't think he looked so hot. I hoped I was right. After he spoke, he just lay there, and watched, without much comment. The TV set was on, with the sound turned down. I thought how it would have been if I had plugged the TV into a socket in his room, instead of on a different line in the attic. She would never have figured it out. There would have been no way to turn off just the intercom alone.

"We'll fix you up in a jiffy," I said.

She stood behind me, watching. I knew she was nervous. He watched with those eyes, breathing sickishly. It got me nervous, too. I lit a cigarette, and uncovered the unit, and had a look.

"Blow a tube, Ruxton?" he said.

"Could be. We'll see."

I went around the house, and made as if I were checking all the units, after I disconnected the one in his room. I tightened the fuse in the fuse box in the utility room. Then I went back and picked up the unit in his room, and said, "Ah-ha! Here it is."

So I soldered a .005 mfd coupling condenser to a grid terminal of a tube socket. The solder flowed like hot gravy. Not a slip-up. It was really a neat job of sloppy work.

I put the unit back together, flipped it on, and let him try it out. Then I turned it off. It would work for approximately ten seconds before heating up enough to expand the metal, make contact, and ground out. The clearance was so close that once it went out, it would stay that way for good.

I looked at him. He was staring at me.

"Questions?" I said.

He didn't say anything, watching me.

"No, Ruxton," he said. "No questions."

I took another look at him, hoped it would be my last, and went into the living room. She was right there, showing me her skirt.

"I can't hang around," I said. "We can't take any chances. Right now is when it's easy to slip up, make some damned fool mistake."

"Please, Jack—hold me."

Well, I held her. I held her tight, and looked over her shoulder at his bedroom door.

I said, "Don't call me unless something unforeseen comes up. Otherwise, I'll read about it in the papers."

"This is it, isn't it, Jack."

"Yeah, that's for sure."

"I mean," she said. "You know, it isn't a bad feeling. I mean, it's exciting. There's so much to come."

"Let's hope it's all things we can handle. Don't get cocky. Keep levelheaded."

"I love you, Jack."

"I love you, too."

"Say my name."

"Shirley."

"It shivers me," she said. "It's going to be rugged, not seeing you."

"That's how it's got to be."

"Jack, I'm all yours. All of me. I just want to be yours."

I said, "You know how it is. Neither of us would be worth a damn, without that money. That's how it is."

"I'm not forgetting that."

I said, "You're sure the money's not tied up, so we can't get at it."

"It's like I told you. There's that in the bank, in cash. He does have some invested, but everything's negotiable. There's not a thing to stew about, believe me."

"And you want to go through with this."

"Why do you say that?"

"Because now's the time to say it."

"I want to go through with it. God, how I want that."

"Okay," I said. "We're on the way. This is it."

I left, then. And, well, there was a look in her eye.

I got to thinking maybe it wouldn't be long before I spotted the story on the obituary page. I sure didn't want to see it on page one.

Somehow I got through that first night. I kept hearing the phone ring. I would sit up in bed and stare at the dark, listening. There would be nothing. Once I got out of bed, tripped over a chair, scrambling for the phone, grabbed it up. "Hello—Hello!"

It hadn't rung. There was nobody on the line. It was just me. Dreaming.

And the next afternoon, about two o'clock, I was in the store, changing some stuff around in the show window. I kept feeling this black shadow from the street. I'd felt it for quite a while, back and forth, but it hadn't meant anything. I looked up and it was Shirley Angela, driving past in the black Imperial, her white face staring at me.

She motioned for me to come out, when she saw me look.

She was double parked, down a couple doors. "I've got to see you. Get in."

"No," I said. "Is it important?"

"Yes." Her face told me that. It was as if somebody had been clubbing her, or something. Not marked up. I mean, behind the eyes, in the expression.

"Meet me on the corner of Fourth and First," I said. "Park the car and walk."

I turned away and went on down to the drugstore and bought cigarettes, then came back to the store. I didn't know what I was doing. I was afraid to speak to anybody, for fear I'd just talk a lot of mishmash. I went straight through the store, and the shop, and out back to the parking lot. I took the car and drove downtown. I had asked her to meet me on one of the busiest corners in town. I parked the car, and walked fast over there. She was walking up and down, waiting, working her fingers on a shiny black purse, as if she were playing a piano.

"Well," I said. "I'll be damned. You downtown, shopping?"

"Don't fool with me, Jack."

I shot it at her. "Make it seem like we met accidentally."

Pedestrians streamed past.

"He wants to go to the hospital."

"What?"

"Doctor Miraglia's there right now," she said. "I told him I had some shopping to do, that I'd only be gone a few minutes. I've been driving up and down past your darned store for over a half an hour."

She was nervous and scared. "Why didn't you call me?"

"You said not to call."

"I told you if something unforeseen...."

She broke in. "All right." She scraped at her lower lip with her teeth. "I was afraid to call, Jack. I didn't know what to do. I thought if I could just catch your eye—I wasn't thinking."

I tried to act calm. "What do you mean, he wants to go to the hospital?"

"He's been at me all day. How good he feels, stuff like that. He wants to go to the hospital for a complete physical check-up."

"Can't the doctor give that to him at home?"

"It's not that. He doesn't carry all the facilities around in his pockets. They use machines on him, all sorts of things."

It hit me hard. It was very bad and for a second there I saw the whole thing exploding soundlessly in our faces. Her face was wrung. "Take it easy," I said. "Try to smile and make it look good. You never know who might come by. I know a lot of people in this town."

"That's not all," she said. "There's more."

"Naturally."

"Doctor Miraglia talked with me privately. He says this is a miracle. He says it's his chance—once he gets Victor to the hospital, he thinks he can talk him into staying there."

I rubbed one hand across my face, hanging onto my jaw.

"Jack." She whispered it tightly. "What will we do?"

"Easy, now," I said. "Here's what you'll have to do. First, you get back there as fast as you can. And be sure to stop at the market and buy some stuff, so it'll look as if you really went shopping."

"Yes. But what—?"

"Ten to one, Miraglia will leave. He'll plan to come back for him. Maybe an ambulance. Anyway, it's up to you to get to Victor. He's always been scared about hospitals. You'll have to make him think that way again. Scare the hell out of him. Only you've got to do it so Miraglia won't get wise. Play it careful—kid him, make it look good. If you fail, we're done."

She didn't speak. She was staring at the front of a jewelry store, thinking. You could almost see the wheels winding up.

"All right," she said. "I think I can do it."

"But be careful."

"Don't worry."

The way she said it, she would scare anybody.

"Jack," she said, looking at me. "I love you so. Why must it be like this?"

"You know why."

"I do love you so."

"Easy. We're on the street," I said. "Now, get moving. And remember, I'm with you every minute."

"It's just that we have so much, so very much, Jack."

"Yeah. Now, get—"

A horn beeped lightly by the curb. It was Mayda Lamphier, driving a dusty Pontiac convertible, with the top down. The maroon paint job was scratched, dented.

I spoke fast to Shirley from the side of my mouth.

"Make it look right. We met on the street."

She looked a little worried, but otherwise okay. We went over to Mayda's car.

"Well," Mayda Lamphier said with a shade of insinuation. "What are you two doing downtown?"

I gave her the story of bumping into each other on the street. She believed it, but made with the eyes anyway. I didn't like any part of it. She possessed that knack of being in the wrong place at the right time.

"I'm shopping," Shirley said. "I'm afraid I'll have to run along. I only have a few minutes. Bye, now."

She was gone before either of us could speak.

"Busy girl," I said.

"Yes, isn't she?" Mayda said. "Can I give you a lift somewhere?"

"I was on my way back to the store. Just had lunch."

"Hop in, then."

Horns blared behind her. She had begun to tie up traffic. We cut off down toward the bay. Things seemed just a little tense. Anything more I might say about "accidentally" meeting Shirley on the street would be punching a flat bag. I let it go and sat there worrying. If Mayda had any suspicions at all, it could go very bad later on.

"How'd you like to take a little ride?" she said.

There was something in her voice. She had on a red skirt. She had allowed it to creep up, revealing an inch of bare thigh above rolled stockings. Her legs were slim and racy looking. Her hair streamed in the wind as she eyed me.

I grinned. "Got to get back to the store."

We stopped for a light. She didn't touch her skirt. She didn't look at me, either.

"I know a nice place," she said. "We could take a quick little ride." She looked at me and smiled with her teeth tight together, and it was in her eyes. Her idea of subtle suggestion was to hit you in the face with a bare breast.

This was a perfect chance to reassure her there was nothing between Shirley and myself. She wasn't Shirley, but on the other hand, she wasn't repulsive, either. If I didn't go with her, she would add things up damned quickly.

"Okay," I said. "Let's. I think I'd like it."

"I know I will."

She drove away from the light. I turned toward her, reached over and ran my palm up her thigh, under her skirt, squeezing the flesh. She began to move her hips and she really laid on that gas pedal.

"Don't," she said. "I can't stand it. Wait'll we park. I'll smash into something."

I took my hand away.

"I couldn't be sure," I said.

"Well, you can be sure, now."

She drove hard and reckless, down along the bay, till we were on the outskirts of town. Then she took a dirt road and parked the car in the first thick clump of trees we reached, along the shore of the bay. She came into my arms with a hot little moan.

We never got out of the front seat of the car. I didn't think about Shirley even once, and we were there over an hour. Sometime along in there, she stripped herself naked, and she sure as hell was starved for it.

She didn't know what she was saying half the time.

"Kiss me," she'd say. Then she'd say, "Marry me, marry me, marry me...." She carried on a lot, and it was a hot time, and it was good.

Finally we just sat there, smoking, staring out at the bay. She talked a little about her husband, and how much she missed him. She said that when I'd come over to fix her TV set that night, it was all she could do not to ask me straight out.

"It would've saved some time," I said.

She laughed. She wasn't half bad, but she scared me a little because she was a wise one. You could see her thinking behind the eyes. Finally she said, "Shirl couldn't give you that—the way we just had. She's too young—she hasn't been around enough."

I didn't say anything. It was then I first thought, What if Shirley ever found out? What if Mayda goes and tells her? It would be just like her.

Only I couldn't say a word. I couldn't tell her to keep her mouth shut.

I checked my watch.

"Cripes," I said. "I've got to get back to the store, right away. I'm late and there's a big deal cooking. I can't afford to miss out."

"Damn," she said. "I thought we could make a night of it."

I told her I was sorry, that I'd like it, too.

"Maybe some other time?" she said.

"We'll try and work something out."

She looked at me and didn't say anything. She got dressed. I couldn't think of anything but Shirley Angela and Victor. Shirley had said Victor felt great. Maybe he was doing calisthenics in his bedroom, waiting to run off to the hospital. And now Mayda. Why had her husband gone off to Alaska at a time like this? Maybe to recuperate.

We didn't talk much on the way back through town. She finally readied the alley behind the shop, drove in, and parked. She obviously knew where the store was. I didn't like that, either.

I got out. She twisted on the seat, and eyed me.

"Shirl's not having all the fun, now," she said.

"Okay. Quit riding me."

"Is she any good?"

"I damned well wouldn't know."

"All right," she said. "I'll stop. I believe you." She smiled, then said. "Will we get together again?"

I grinned at her. "It's possible," I said.

"You know it," she said.

I told her I had to get into the shop. I banged the car with my fist, and turned away.

"I'm not forgetting," she called.

I waved back at her. She drove off. As soon as she

was out of sight, I walked down the alley, hailed a cab, and had the driver take me downtown to where I'd parked my car.

Driving back to the store, I went through two red lights. I had to know what went with Victor. I couldn't go out there. I didn't know what to do. There wasn't anything I could do but wait.

At twelve-thirty that night the phone rang.

"Jack? I had to call you."

"Glad you did." I'd just made up my mind I would have to go out there and rap on her window, or something. "How is it?"

Her voice sounded pooped. "It's all right, I think. I kidded him about the way he'd been acting. It wasn't easy, Jack. It was a little pitiful. He felt so great, and I had to tear him down. It worked, though. He told Miraglia he'd changed his mind. I thought he was going to have another attack."

"He didn't let on you'd changed his mind for him?"

"No. He's too egotistical for that. But Miraglia was angry. He hardly spoke to me. I tried to tell him I'd done everything I could to keep Victor thinking the right way. He left in a snit."

"Where you calling from?"

"The house. But it's all right. He can't hear me."

"Are you all right, Shirley?"

"It's just I want to see you so badly."

"I know."

"I hope you know. Jack—I love you so."

"We can't see each other now. We shouldn't even be talking on the phone."

"Thank God he's going to die. Maybe you don't want to see me. Maybe it's only the money. Maybe after we do it, you'll only want the money."

"Christ almighty," I said.

"Well—?"

"Shirley, please."

"All right. Only you can't begin to imagine."

"Yes, I can. Take it easy and hang on."

"All right, Jack."

"We'd better cut this off."

"Jack?"

She had something else on her mind.

She said. "How did you make out with Mayda?"

My heart struck hard twice in my chest. "Make out?"

"When she drove you back to the store, I mean."

I tried to tell myself there was nothing strange about her tone of voice. "She just drove me back, is all—then I went down and got my car."

"You didn't go anywhere with her, did you?"

"Hell, no—of course not. Why should I?"

"Don't be stupid, Jack."

I didn't say anything. I couldn't.

She got louder. "Jack—tell me."

"She just drove me back to the store. She's not suspicious, or anything."

"I don't mean that."

All I could think was, Could Mayda have said something?

Shirley said, "I saw Mayda early this evening. She acted kind of strange. She kept talking about you, all the time. Jack—if you ever—!"

"Take it easy. You know better than that."

I could hear her breathing. It wouldn't take much and she would blow up.

"Shirley?" I said.

"Yes."

"I love you, Shirley. Will you remember that?"

"All right."

"Are you all right?"

"Yes. I'll be all right."

"Just get that stuff out of your head, Shirley."

"I'm sorry. I couldn't help it."

"I wouldn't lie to you," I said. "Ever. Okay?"

"Yes. I won't think about it." She didn't speak for a time. I could hear her breathing. Then her voice came across the line, touched with desperation, a kind of dry whisper. "I'm going to work on him, Jack," she said. "I'm going to work on him right now. I can't stand it any longer."

Eight

By the time the next afternoon crept across the face of the clock, I was in pretty bad shape. I needed a drink. I was afraid to start hitting the bottle. It would be too easy to lose count and go all the way. I chain-smoked cigarettes. I wandered around the store in a fog, trying to keep out of things because I knew I might foul up somewhere. Luckily, I had the place set up so I could come and go freely, acting as a general overseer. Louis Sneed and Pete Stallsworth were good repair men, or I would have been in a fix. I had a middle-aged blonde, a Mrs. Noxton, on the front desk, handling the phone, doing file work, and so forth. All she ever thought about was getting off work and hitting her favorite cocktail lounge to sop up Martinis. She was a wise one, but she could mind her own business, and that's what counted. It was why she'd been here as long as she had.

All sorts of things came to mind. The big thing was I began to know we should have had some set time, place, or way, to contact each other. It was all right for her. She was there, on the spot. She knew what was going on. I had no idea how things were. It was like hanging by your upper lip to a high diving board over an empty swimming pool.

The later it got, the worse it got.

For all I knew, Miraglia was out there now, closing Victor's eyes, and nodding sadly. With Shirley pulling the weep act. I wondered if she could weep. I wondered if she would weep.

Maybe she would just rear back and scream with laughter.

I knew I had to stop thinking. I couldn't. I would get to thinking of Victor gasping for air, and I would breathe deeply. It was as if I couldn't get enough air myself.

I tried concentrating on the money. What it could do, what it could buy. It just didn't cut through the mood. It was so much money, I'd never be able to grasp the reality until I could actually grasp the money in my hand.

To top it off, we had a busy day at the store. They poured in and out all day, looking at TV sets, inspecting a couple of tired old short-wave receivers I'd blurbed as perfect for tracking satellites, listening to hi-fi systems, stereo tape recorders, and the like. I talked to them. My mind wandered. I couldn't get anything straight.

Finally I went off into a corner behind a screen backing a display of phonographs, and sat in a chair, smoking. I kept thinking about Shirley. I kept trying not to wonder how it would turn out. A hopeless way to think, like Tolstoy saying to go in a corner and try not to think about a white bear. Christ. How to flip.

After a while it was time to eat something again, so I walked down to the drugstore and fooled around with a ham sandwich and a glass of milk. It was dark outside. Neons glowed in the streets. Cars hissed up and down on their way to parties, maybe, good times, or just home to the one-eyed monster, and the evening paper.

I started up the street toward the store, still thinking about Shirley. It hit me. Maybe it had been there all the time. I'd been trying to ignore it. Anyway, my mind was like pancake batter. I'd been worrying about Shirley going soft. It was me we had to worry about— because what was really in the back of my mind was the feeling that we had rushed into this too fast. Why force it? We knew how we felt about each other. What we had. We knew it would last. Money would do that.

So why not just let it coast along? Let Victor die the way he would die, in time. We could stand it, couldn't we?

I had to see her.

If I talked with her, she'd think the same. He could eventually wind up in the hospital, and Shirley and I could see each other all we wanted. It would be on the up and up. He'd croak natural, and everything would be perfect. Except we would have to wait.

Maybe she'd been thinking this way, too. Just scared to say anything, because we'd gone too far. At least, we could talk it over. I could sound her out and see.

It was a kind of relief. So it would take longer. Maybe not. So what? We wouldn't have worries riding us.

I found myself running up the alley. I slowed to a walk, went over and took one of the trucks, and headed across town. I had no excuse to see her. Suddenly I realized I didn't need an excuse. It was all aboveboard; a strange feeling.

Nearing her place, I felt better. I began to whistle and sing, driving through the dark streets under streetlights. The tensions vanished.

I sang. Just anything. I let it rip out across the night. It made me feel better than ever.

In front of her house. I parked by the curb. There were no lights that I could see. I started for the porch, then thought maybe she would be in her room. I decided to take the path around back and surprise her.

I started along the stepping stones that led along the side of the house. Bright white light fell in a broad swath out on the yard. It came from Victor's bedroom window.

I looked in. It was only a quick glance, in passing. I was in a hurry to get out back. I paused by the open window. The way he looked, I knew something was wrong.

Victor was propped up in the bed, on one arm, leaning toward the bedroom doorway, his head cocked, listening. He looked sick, and weak as hell. His skin was an ugly gray color. I heard the way he breathed. It was ghastly.

I stood there a moment. My heart rocked. He dropped back flat on the bed, mouth open, making gasping sounds, and stared up at the TV set. The set was on with the sound off. A musical production was on the screen; dancing girls and prancing boys. Big glass chandeliers flew through the air across an enormous stage set.

Victor Spondell reached to the bed table, and flipped on the intercom unit. He listened. Voices burst loudly through the speaker, carrying to me through the open window.

Shirley and Mayda Lamphier.

"For goodness' sake, Mayda," Shirley said. "You must be crazy to think such a thing."

Mayda Lamphier's voice was strained. There was a quality of awed and hesitant fright in her tone. "I thought I *was* crazy," she said. "Shirley—" Her voice was shaded with pleading. "I know, believe me, I know what you've been going through. Anybody would flip, taking care of that old geezer. But, not this, Shirley."

She ceased talking. Neither of them spoke. I couldn't move from where I stood. I wanted to move, but something held me there. I knew what it was. It was doom.

Shirley spoke. Her voice was level now, and deadly.

"How did you ever form such a conclusion?"

"Oh, Shirl!"

"How, Mayda?"

"The telephone," Mayda Lamphier said. "We're on a party line, remember?" She paused, then went on. "I shouldn't have. I've been lonely, I guess—that must account for it. I was going to make a call, last night around twelve. I picked up the receiver and you were talking to that Ruxton character. I heard everything you said, Shirl—everything. It was obvious, only I still couldn't believe it. I watched you through the window—how you spoke to that old man."

Shirley was cool now. "What are you going to do?"

"I thought you were just maybe on the make for this Ruxton. But, not this—not doing—killing—" Her voice rose. "Murdering that old man! Shirl, I'm trying to help you. That Ruxton's nothing but a cheap bum. Can't you see that?" She ceased, then, "I shouldn't've waited...."

There was a pause. Nobody spoke. My heart was like a bass drum, slamming inside my chest. Victor Spondell was half up in bed again, straining. His eyes were wild. If Mayda told Shirley about what we'd done, what then?

They didn't speak. I knew then. The intercom had quit, just as I'd planned it to quit. Victor reached for it. He struck it with his hand, eyes glaring toward the bedroom door, mouth gaping.

I turned and ran along the walk toward the front of the house.

I ran straight into Grace.

I smashed into her before I could stop. I don't

know. I was pretty close to insanity at that moment. Maybe it was like being shot in the heart. I couldn't even speak. She had on a white dress and I smelled the gin. I thrust her away, and there was a kind of screaming inside me.

"I followed you, Jack."

"What are you doing here?"

"I followed you. You don't think I'd really leave town, the way you've been treating me? You don't really think that, do you? I knew you had another woman, Jack—seeing her. I knew that's what it was. I wasn't good enough, was I? So I've been following you. She lives right here, doesn't she? She married? She sneaking out to meet you? Don't try to kid me, Jack. I know."

I didn't know what to do with her. I had to get rid of her. Everything was wild and off-kilter. Time counted. She was just drunk enough to be belligerent. Grace could be belligerent. I turned her around on the walk.

"You find your car," I said, "and get out of here. Fast. You're not fouling me up."

"Fouling you up?" She gave a short bitter laugh. "You've got a woman here. You think I don't know?"

I kept my voice down. "You're wrong, Grace. I had a service call at the shop. I left the store ten minutes ago. They're having TV trouble here."

"What were you doing, staring in that window?"

"I wasn't staring in any window, Grace. You're

drunk and you're not fouling me up. Move," I said.

She balked. She pushed back against me. I figured I would fly apart, the way I felt. She turned, with her face squinched up, and cursed me. She was too loud.

"You expect me to believe that?" She said. "Damn you, Jack—you dirty liar!"

I hit her. I hit her so hard she ran sideways off across the lawn, and fell in a heap. I went over and yanked her to her feet. I hit her again. I let her have it hard. Then I turned her, with her sobbing and moaning, and bent her arm up behind her back and ran her staggering out on the lawn. Her car was parked behind the truck. It was a yellow Buick hardtop.

It had me nuts, wondering what went on in that house.

"Now," I said. "You get in that car and get out of here. You come around me again, I'll smash your jaw. Get going."

She stood there with her face full of wrath.

I opened the door on the driver's side, and flung her under the wheel and slammed the door shut.

"Go," I said. "Fast."

Her face was something out of a comic book. She looked crazy.

"I swear it, Grace. You come around me again, it's a promise. Stay away from me."

She was sobbing and talking to herself. She kept choking and trying to swallow. She wanted to say

something, but she was so mad she never got it out.
She started the engine, shoved the car into reverse,
backed away from the truck, slammed it into low, and
shot past me. She barreled down the street with the
gas pedal to the floor.

I ran back to the house, down the side walk of
stepping stones. Victor Spondell wasn't in his bed. I
saw him, clinging to the door jamb. He hung there
like a kind of ghost in ballooning white pajamas, his
hands clawing at the woodwork.

I ran around back. Shirley's bedroom light was on.
The kitchen was bright. I went up on the back porch
as softly as I could.

The kitchen door was open. What I saw in there
was like some crazy scene out of a movie. The bright
neon kitchen light shone down on Shirley and Mayda.
Shirley's face was puffed with anger, tinged with red
against that white pallor, in an effort to keep herself
under control. She wasn't doing a good job. There
was little she could do. The cat was out of the bag,
and running. There was sly scheming in her eyes.
Desperation showed in the taut shape of her mouth.
She wore the yellow housecoat I'd seen before.

"Just exactly what *do* you intend to do, then?"
Shirley said. Her tone was flat. "You'd have one tough
time trying to prove anything like this, Mayda."

I hugged the porch shadows. Mayda Lamphier's
back was to me. Shirley hadn't seen me. Mayda's
shoulders were tense under a white sweater, her

hands clenched into the dark fabric of her skirt, at her hips.

"You won't listen to me, will you," she said.

Shirley didn't speak. She stood by the sink. The kitchen table was between them.

What happened then, I would never forget. There was something more than horrifying about it.

"All right," Mayda said. "I've tried." She half turned toward the porch door.

Shirley's voice rose. "Where are you going?"

Mayda turned toward her again. She didn't speak. There must have been some readable expression in her face, because Shirley reacted sharply.

"You won't tell anybody!" Shirley said. "You *won't!*"

"Won't I, though…?"

Mayda turned and moved fast for the porch. I could never let her pass me. I worked on instinct now, and stepped out in front of her.

"You." It scared her. She stopped, staring at me, her eyes wide and round. "You," she said again.

Shirley was clawing through a kitchen drawer over by the sink. She whirled, running, the yellow housecoat billowing. She saw me.

"Jack!"

Mayda made a stab at getting past me. I grabbed her shoulders, facing her. She struggled, making hurt sounds in her throat. I shoved her back toward the kitchen, and there was a kind of savage desperation inside me.

"Let's talk this over," I said.

Shirley came full tilt across the kitchen. I didn't see the knife until it arched in a vicious slant at Mayda Lamphier's back. I tried to fling Mayda aside. I heard her grunt with pain.

"Don't let her go!" Shirley said.

Mayda lurched free over against the kitchen wall.

"You crazy fool," I said to Shirley.

She stared at Mayda, one hand at her mouth. Her eyes were like glass.

I thrust her out of the way and stepped toward Mayda. I was scared all the way now. I had no idea whether she'd told Shirley about what we'd done in her car, down by the bay.

Mayda Lamphier moved away from the wall, watching us. She tried to speak. Her hands both reached up behind her back. Her face was filled more with shock than pain. She broke, running for the kitchen door that led into the dinette.

I saw the knife sticking out of her back. It was a carving knife, and the blade was in to the hilt. She kept struggling to reach it with her hands. The back of her white sweater was a sheet of dark blood. She stopped, swayed, and fell to the floor.

She said, "No," sharply.

I went over to her. I was conscious of Victor Spondell standing in the doorway.

"Jack," Shirley said. "Is she all right?"

Somehow, from the way Shirley spoke, I knew

Mayda hadn't told her about what we'd done. Mayda Lamphier was dying. For only a moment, she was dying. Her eyes looked up at me with awe and confusion from the cramped position of neck and head. Then she was dead.

I would never know why she hadn't told.

That didn't matter now. What mattered was that she was dead and the ball was rolling.

"I was just trying to stop her," Shirley said. "I couldn't let her go."

"That's right," I said. "You couldn't."

I looked up at Victor Spondell.

I was shriveled up like a weed inside, now.

Spondell turned dazedly and stumbled toward the living room, his white pajamas ballooning.

"Stop him," Shirley said.

I stood up, and looked at her. I heard myself speak.

"It's all right," I said. "You couldn't do anything else. There was nothing else to do."

She nodded numbly. I heard the telephone dial.

"Victor," I said.

I turned fast and went in there. He was in the living room, dialing on the phone. He saw me and went all to pieces. I yanked the phone out of his hand and slapped it on the cradle. He fell back against the wall, trying to get his breath.

I guess maybe it was right about here that the whole thing began to turn into a nightmare.

I stood there looking at Victor Spondell. He had to die. It was either him, or Shirley and me.

You go into a confused state. You do things you know have to be done. It's all very crazy. You know you're doing hellishly wrong things. You know you can't stop doing them, because the minute you stop you'll wash away with the sands. You're a swimmer in a riptide, fighting toward a receding shore.

So details were like that. Swarming in my brain. Victor Spondell had to die. Something had to be done about Mayda Lamphier's body. Miraglia had to be called. The intercom unit had to be checked. I had to post Shirley on what to say. I had to figure what to do with Mayda's body. The money had to be collected.... I would have to get my story straight for Miraglia, and maybe even the Law. Grace was out there someplace, God only knew where, maybe looking in a window now. I had to get rid of the truck before somebody saw it out front. A hundred things were suddenly riding me.

Her whisper came from behind me.

"What will we do, Jack?"

Victor Spondell was sliding down the wall, slowly. He watched me, trying to speak, unable to. He slid down the wall and sprawled on the floor, eyebrows bristling.

"He heard you," I said. "Over the intercom. He heard everything. Why in Christ didn't we think of the telephone? A party line. An obvious, tired old business like that?"

I looked at her. She raised one hand. It smeared on her chin. Then she saw the hand and reacted violently. It was a sight I would never forget.

"Wash your hand—hurry up!"

"What'll we do, Jack?"

"Wash the hand."

I turned and looked at Victor Spondell. She gave a little gasp and started for the kitchen. She stopped in the dinette, then turned and went into her room. I heard the water running in her bathroom.

Victor was crawling along the rug, toward the front of the house. He was saying things. I couldn't make out what the words were. I went over and stood in front of him. His hands clawed at my shoes. He stopped and lay there, panting. He looked up at me, craning his neck. His mouth was a black panting hole, the eyes all gone to hell with fear. He collapsed on the floor. You could see the back of his pajamas, up between his shoulder blades, moving in and out like a bellows, with the way he tried to breathe.

"Mask," he gasped. "Get—air. Oxygen—mask."

I didn't move. I looked down at him, hearing him, but I couldn't move.

Shirley came back. She stood off across the room staring at Victor with a curious expression on her face. It was as if she couldn't bear what she saw—but you could tell she was going to bear it, anyway.

"We've got to get him in the bedroom," I said.

She didn't speak. I looked at her again. She had both hands clenched in front of her, holding her thumbs like a little girl. She looked like a little girl, standing there.

Anxious and confused.

I leaned down, grabbed Victor under the shoulders, and started dragging him toward the bedroom. "Shirley," I said. "Find something that won't be missed around the house. An extra blanket would be best. Go in the kitchen and mop up every last speck of blood, and get Mayda wrapped in the blanket."

I kept on dragging Victor. Shirley didn't move.

"Get going!" I said.

"I can't go in there."

"You've got to. We'll have to move fast."

She clutched at her face with one hand. "I can't."

"All right. Help me with him."

She moved slowly after me as I hauled Victor into the bedroom. He was moaning and gasping. I caught him by the arms, and slung him half up on the bed, then flung his legs up. He lay there writhing and twisting, his hands like claws, the tendons sticking out. His eyes glared toward the rack where the oxygen tanks stood. I went over to Shirley. "Stay with him," I told her. "Don't leave him for a second."

"What are you going to do?"

"Get rid of her."

"How?"

"I'm not sure yet."

She kind of leaped in against me, her arms around me. I could feel how tense she was. "Say you love me."

I kissed her.

"Say you love me, Jack!"

"I love you. You know I love you. Would I be doing any of this if I didn't love you?"

She looked up at me. Her eyes were very wide.

"Shirley," I said. "We've got to move fast. I think I'll get her car—take her someplace, and fake a wreck. I don't know yet."

"If they find her—they'll see the knife wound."

"Yeah. I've got to fix that."

"Jack, I didn't want anything like this to happen."

I pushed her away. "Get in there with him."

"What should I do?"

"Keep him there till I get back. If the phone rings, answer it. You'll know what to say to whoever calls."

She stood there staring at Victor's bedroom doorway. You could hear him in there. Dying.

Nine

Somehow, I did what I had to do.

I carried a casting rod and a couple of plugs in the truck. Sometimes, driving around town on calls, I stopped by different lakes, and had a few tries for bass. It would have to be my alibi now. I drove the truck six blocks from the Spondell house. There was a lake I knew of. I parked the truck, shielding it as best I could in a copse of cedar. It was one of the chances I'd have to take. My explanation, if it ever came to that, would be that Miss Angela had called for TV service. After I left her place, I drove to the lake and made a few casts for fish along the shore. Because the truck might be spotted. It could easily have been seen at Shirley's. Grace had seen it. It was weak business, but maybe it was weak enough to be believable.

I dogged it back to Shirley's. She was in the bedroom with Victor. She got me a blanket. I cleaned the kitchen floor, and the carving knife. I scrubbed the knife with a brush and kitchen cleanser, and did the same with the floor after I had wrapped the body in the blanket.

I was so worried I couldn't see straight, and I knew I had to keep calm.

Mayda Lamphier was still warm. I knew pretty well what I would do.

"She'll be found," Shirley said. "They'll suspect something."

"Nobody's going to suspect anything. They may never find her."

"Victor's dying."

I didn't say anything. I hardly knew what I was doing. "Go back in there with him. Do whatever you feel you should do." I looked at her. "Only don't give him any air. I'll be back as soon as I can."

She avoided looking at the blanket-wrapped body. "I'm scared, Jack."

"I know."

I waited till she went in there with him. I could hear him again. I hoisted what was left of Mayda Lamphier on my shoulder and went out back. The yard was dark. I took her across the lawn, and through the hedge into her driveway where her convertible was parked, and laid her across the seat. Lights were on in her living room.

I got under the wheel, backed the convertible out of the drive, and left that place.

Somebody had to see her car; somebody who knew the car. I drove around the blocks nearby, trying to think.

I recalled a gas station on the corner of the main highway leading south, not far from this residential section. In all probability, Mayda Lamphier had used it at some time or other. Possibly regularly. It was close enough to her home.

I went that way. Neons glowed brightly over the station. An attendant was out front under the marquee, taking care of a customer.

With the gas pedal to the floor, I swerved the car wildly in toward the station, then back onto the highway, and wailed the horn. The attendant couldn't possibly make out who was driving the car. He turned sharply, then waved and shouted something. I figured he did know the car, and it was what I wanted. Even if he didn't know the car, he would remember it. I went on, driving like that, swerving from one side of the road to the other. A truck approached from the opposite direction. I cut directly in front of it. The driver slammed the brakes, and rode the horn. I brought the convertible back at the last minute, knowing he would remember, and that it had been seen by the gas station attendant, and the customer, too. It was good enough.

I opened the convertible up and held it, till I was about eight miles down the road, then took a bisecting country road, and came back toward town again, until I found what I was looking for. I figured it to be about a mile or slightly more from Shirley's place.

There was a stretch of old canal beside the road. The road itself was a dark stretch of potholed, high-humped macadam; a back route to town. Trees grew

profusely along the canal banks. I had fished the
water, and knew it was plenty deep.

It would have to be a fast job. The road was seldom
traveled, but that didn't mean no one would come
along. If I were spotted, if the convertible were seen
out here, stopped on the road, we were done.

I parked the car on the road, and got out for a
quick inspection. Finally I found what I wanted.

What happened now had to be perfect.

There was no sound of a car. The night was inert.
Not even a cricket. No wind. I found a long, loose
limb, took off shoes, socks and trousers, and waded in
the water close to the old canal bank. So far as I could
make out by testing with the limb, the water was very
deep—well over the top of any car. It was turgid
water, scummed with weeds and surface moss.

Dressing, I returned to the car. Still no sounds.

What I did then was bred of desperation and the
knowledge of what could happen if and when Mayda
Lamphier's body ever might be recovered. It was
something I could never have done again.

The convertible top was up. First I unwrapped the
blanket, and put it safely in some bushes on the canal
bank. Then I stood on the rear deck of the car, and
jumped on the convertible top. The canvas top
ripped. Steel stays bent. But not enough. I unhooked
the top, and using all my might, managed to bend the
steel forms under the canvas out of shape, and I

finally snapped loose a single steel rod from the driver's side.

I slung the body under the wheel. The body had to stay with the car. I couldn't bind it in there with rope. I jammed an arm between the steering post and the dashboard, and did my best to fasten one of the feet under the gas pedal. The other leg I twisted up around the steering post and propped under the dash, as a lever to hold the body. Then I shoved the head between the twin spokes of the steering wheel. It didn't look as if it would ever come loose.

Then the bad part. The knife wound. I took the steel support from the convertible top, got it set, closed my eyes, and drove it into her back through the spot where the knife blade had stuck.

I heard the sound of a car's engine. It was distant, but it was tearing up road space, whining in the night.

I had wanted to take my time. I couldn't.

Starting the engine, I reached for the gas pedal. Her foot was underneath, so I couldn't press it down. It was a serious flaw.

Back on the road, I saw the car's headlights shining above tree tops. The oncoming car was rounding a series of S curves about a half mile away.

There was nothing to do. I yanked at the foot. It wouldn't come free. I heard myself cursing. It had me out of my head. There wasn't time now. I reached for the hand throttle, yanked it out, and set it. The gas pedal went down enough so the engine was wound up. But if they found the throttle pulled out, it would be obvious what had been done—or at least suspicious.

The car wasn't in gear.

I let loose the throttle. I was completely out of my mind now. I pulled the shift lever into drive, and yanked the throttle out, and stuck with the car as it bucked and began slowly to move off the road toward the canal. It was all fouled up. I saw the other car coming along the road, then.

I yanked the throttle all the way out, twisted it into lock position. The car shot toward the canal. I jumped and slammed the door and let it go, and knew I'd made a worse slip still as the convertible leaped off the bank and struck the water. The headlights were off. They had to be on.

It didn't make much of a splash. It hit and slid down into the water, with the engine going. Waves splashed against the shore, and the engine had quit.

I hugged the ground by some brush. The oncoming car swept past, going like hell, headlights glaring across the night. The canal was frothing white where the convertible had gone under.

The sound of the car on the road gradually diminished.

I looked at the darkness, and knew I had to go in that water. I had to go down there and make sure. I would never know, unless I did.

The headlights had to be turned on. The hand throttle had to be released. The foot had to be freed from beneath the accelerator.

I stripped and walked into the water. The water was cold. The night was black, and the mud banks under my feet suddenly gave sharply away. I kept my feet, walking directly toward where the car had gone under. I slid abruptly down the slimy, steep bank to my chin. I took another step and went under. Holding my breath, I fought toward the car, smashed into it with my face against steel. It was deep. I hauled myself down fast to the dashboard, found the headlight knob, yanked it out. The lights didn't come on; shorted out. But I had that much accomplished. Then I released the hand throttle.

I couldn't stay under any longer. Out of breath, I fought for the surface, came up overly conscious of the possibilities of alligators in the water now.

I didn't want to go down there again. I had to. I took another deep breath, and dove. I caught some of the convertible top, and pulled myself down to the car seat. She was still jammed the way I'd fixed her. I located her foot under the gas pedal, braced myself, and tore it free.

When I came up, a car's headlights had brightened the night, moving slowly along the canal roadway. I ducked into the water again, waiting. When I came up, the car had passed. I swam for the bank, crawled up on the mud and lay there.

The sensation of being trapped was very bad now. Of what we had done. Of what I was doing. There was a moment of realization of how life had been before I'd met Shirley Angela, and I lay there on the muddy bank, and began to laugh. The laughter was bad, and it stopped as abruptly as it had begun.

I got sick.

Finally I lay there on the bank, panting. My head ached. The whole thing was an impossible business. But it had happened. And it had only begun happening. All I'd accomplished was to take care of one little point that wasn't even supposed to have happened. A tiny flaw. A diseased speck in what lay ahead.

I got down into the water again and scrubbed the mud and scum away, then came up the bank and dressed.

After that I went over the ground carefully, wishing I had a flashlight, but making what moonlight there was do. I smoothed out my footprints, and obliterated the tire tracks enough so they wouldn't be noticed, but would still be there.

Then I started down the road.

I'd taken maybe a hundred paces, when I remembered the blanket.

I ran back. I couldn't find the place where I'd hidden it. I couldn't even find the place where the convertible had gone over into the canal.

Another car passed. I hid again, then went on

looking. Finally I found the blanket. I rolled it up tightly, and stood there. I couldn't figure what to do with it.

Then I got to laughing again. For a minute or two, I couldn't stop. It wasn't really laughing. It was a kind of loud shouting. Then it stopped.

I started down the road with the blanket rolled up under my arm. Mayda Lamphier's death blood was soaked into the cloth. I didn't know what to do with it.

It was nutty. Everything was in order. Everything had to be in order all the way down the line. Except for this damned blanket.

I couldn't burn it. I couldn't tear it to shreds, and float the stuff away on the wind. If I threw it into the canal, somebody would find it. A fisherman would find it, maybe. So for a moment I was blocked solid.

There was only one thing to do. Bury it.

I cut off the road, on the opposite side from the canal. The land was wooded with pine. I walked and stumbled through the woods, until I thought I was far enough in. It would look different in daylight. Maybe I was in somebody's back yard.

The hell with it. I dug with both hands. I scraped out a hole about four feet deep in the sandy, mucky soil, jammed the blanket down there, and covered it. I littered the spot with dried pine needles and leaves and ruck from surrounding ground, then hiked it back to the road.

Once on the road again, I ran.

Ten

"He's dead, Jack."

She was like a hunk of marble. The only thing that gave away what was going on inside her was her eyes. I didn't say anything. I went into the bedroom and looked at him, there on the bed.

His knees were buckled, with those big feet sticking out, and he was on his side. His hands were shaped into large claws, the tendons in shadowed relief. The hands were stretched out at arm's length, toward the oxygen tanks. But his face really got me.

From the neck up, he was choked with a kind of rich purple, blotched with blues and grays. The eyes were bugged right out of his head. It looked as if you would have to punch them back in order to close the lids. The mouth was stretched open as if he were screaming like an animal, with the purple lips drawn back away from the teeth as if they'd been stapled into his jaws.

All that eagle-like arrogance was gone now.

"He died a few minutes before you came, Jack."

Her voice was flat and there was fear.

Well, I thought. This is what you wanted.

The bright white light glared down on the room.

The oxygen mask was on the bed. The TV set was still turned on with the sound off. A guy on the screen was sneaking down an alley. It was raining in the alley.

I knew then that I hadn't really wanted Victor to die. Only it was too late.

Maybe it was all wrong. Maybe we'd gone too far. But I knew this, too—it couldn't be undone. So now was the time to make it pay.

I heard Shirley say something. She grabbed me with both arms. "Oh, Jack...."

All I thought of was the money. I didn't want it that way. Here she was, scared stiff, like a little kid, wanting me to comfort her, needing me, wanting me to say something to her so she wouldn't feel so bad. And all I could think of was the money.

It was strange. There were bright little moments of realization, knowing what was really happening. And with those brief interims came a hopeless trapped feeling I'd never had before.

I thrust her away, holding her shoulders. Her face didn't look too good.

"We've got to have everything absolutely straight," I said. "Are the volume controls turned up on the outside speakers?"

"Jack. He kept crying for air. He lasted and lasted. I stood there and watched him. I taunted him, Jack. I was crazy—I must have been crazy. I just stood there.

I couldn't move. I didn't want to move—just to see him die."

For a moment I thought she was going to crack.

"Easy, now, Shirley."

I remembered something: I went back into Victor's bedroom and checked the intercom unit. Sure enough, it was turned off. He must have turned it off after it stopped working. I turned it back on and up to full-volume. His was a master control. I flipped open all the remotes.

I went back to the living room. She hadn't moved.

"Your story, Shirley—can you make it all right?"

She stood there with one hand clamped over her mouth, the round eyes staring at me.

"Shirley," I said. My voice cracked a little. "I've got to get out of here. Remember. You were out back, sitting by the Gulf. You didn't hear anything." I pulled her hand away from her face and said slowly and harshly, "Will you get everything straight?"

"Yes. Jack. Mayda—?"

"Never mind Mayda. Don't even think about her. Forget she was ever around here. The less you know, the…"

"I've got to know."

"Okay." I told her about Mayda, thinking again how if she'd ever found out about Mayda and me, things wouldn't even be this good. "Now, forget her." I wanted to forget her.

She said, "It's all wrong, Jack."

"Don't think it for a second, Shirley. Now's when we need strength. We're in it. There's no backing out now." I glanced at the bedroom. "Listen," I said. "Already we're wasting time. You've got to call Miraglia now."

"I called him, Jack."

"You what?"

"I called him maybe five minutes ago, before you came."

I didn't speak.

She said, "I knew I had to. It wouldn't look right unless I called. I had to do what was right. I didn't know when you'd get back. I knew if you came back when he was here, you'd see his car out front. It's all right, Jack—don't look like that!"

I still said nothing.

She said, "It's all right, Jack. It's all over. Say you love me."

I stared at her. "I've got to get out of here."

"I told the doctor what had happened, how I didn't hear him. And when I came in, he was having a bad attack. I told him the oxygen didn't seem to do any good. I gave him a nitroglycerin pill, for his heart— but it didn't seem to do any good, either. I said Victor fought the oxygen when I tried to help him. He said he'd known something like this would happen—that he'd be right over."

"Listen," I said. "Don't call me. On your life. Don't try to contact me. I'll contact you." I took her in my arms, then, because I needed somebody to hang onto, too. Only I let go of her right away, because it didn't do any good. It was as if I were in a dream, and none of this had happened. Only it had happened. I knew I hadn't meant it to happen. Isn't that what they always say afterward? The whole business tumbled down over me like a big black wet tent.

Her eyes were glassy.

"Jack, don't go and leave me all alone. I couldn't stand it."

"You'll have to stand it. Right now is when we'll both have to stand everything. Listen, the big thing now is getting that money. You hear? There's no telling what'll happen now. It won't be easy. It's going to be close, believe me. Start on that money as soon as you can. I'll reach you, somehow."

"But we'll have to wait for the money. There's always a waiting period."

"Yeah." I wasn't even thinking about what she said. "We've got to be careful." I ceased talking. Things were happening too fast. A car had pulled up out front, and I heard the low moan of a distant siren. Almost immediately a car door slammed.

"I'm all alone, Jack. You're leaving me with this all alone. I can't stand it. I don't know whether I can do it."

"You've got to do it!"

Her face took on that stunned expression. I thought she might start bawling. I shook her, listening, and knowing I had to run for it.

"I'll get in touch with you," I said.

I turned and ran for the kitchen.

"Jack—*please!*"

She was nuts. There was the sound of another car out front. Maybe an ambulance. Voices. I went on through the kitchen. It looked clean. The carving knife was on the kitchen table. She called softly again. As I went across the back porch, somebody pounded on the front door.

I ran across the back lawn with the hounds of hell after me, thinking how she might crack. She couldn't crack. She had to do it right, damn her. If she made even one mistake, it would be all they'd need.

I was sick and scared. I wished to God I'd never met Shirley Angela....

There hadn't been time to really know what had happened back there with her.

It began to get to me as I reached the truck. The whole thing really got to me, then. I slid under the wheel and sat there and shook. I cried. I cursed Shirley Angela, and myself, and Victor Spondell, and Doctor Miraglia, and Mayda Lamphier, and her god-damned husband for being away in Alaska.

And all the time I was like that, I knew I wanted the money. Behind all the fear and the knowing, was the thought of that money. It was a curse. It was inside, from way back in my childhood, and I knew nothing would ever tear it up out of me, either. It had been my chance, and I'd taken it. That was that. There wasn't anything else, now—just get that money.

I had hardly started back toward town with the truck when the rest of it began gnawing. How had she made out? What had she said? Did Miraglia believe her? Had he any reason to doubt what she said? But he wouldn't have. There was no reason. Victor was dead, and he'd said himself that he had expected something like this to happen.

Then I wondered if that was what Miraglia really meant. Or was I reading something into it that I wanted there?

I knew I'd have to go home. I would wait. How in all hell could I stand it? Not knowing what was going on? I'd told her not to contact me. That had been wrong. I should have told her to contact me as soon as she saw how things were shaping up.

What was it she'd said about having to "wait for the money?"

I turned the truck around and drove past the spot where I'd hidden it in the copse of cedar, by the lake. I knew I shouldn't go anywhere near her place, but I couldn't stop myself. I drove down the street before I reached her street, a block away, trying to look across the block, between the houses. I couldn't see anything.

I had to know something. Anything. Just to look at the house, see it—know it was there. See if Miraglia was still there.

I drove around the block and came back up her street. There were no cars parked out front, no sign of anything. The house was dark.

She wasn't there. I sensed the house's emptiness.

Well, it made things worse. I turned at the end of the block and drove back past the house again. It looked black and cold. It looked dead.

Next door, in Mayda Lamphier's living room, the lights still burned. And out there in the night, cold water flowed across her dead eyes and through her hair.

I drove back to the store, picked up my car, and headed for home.

The minute that apartment door closed behind me, I was a goner. I stood there in the darkness for about a half a second, then I jumped for the light switch. I got the lights on, and began pacing.

In the kitchen, I stood by the sink with the water turned on, a glass in my hand. I set the glass down. The next thing, I was in the bedroom, undressing. The water was still running. I went out there, turned it off, and came back and sat on the edge of the bed.

I tried to take a shower. I was under the water for maybe ten seconds, then outside the shower stall, listening. Had the phone rung?

Well, you just wait in the bright silence.

I began to pray the phone would ring.

In the kitchen again, I got out a fifth of gin, and poured a slug down, straight from the bottle. I set the bottle on the drainboard, turned, and just made it to the bathroom in time. That gin bounced like a tennis ball.

But I was persistent. I went back and poured some more down, and that stayed. Only it didn't do any good.

I went to bed, turned off the light. Like a shot, I was sitting up in bed. They would find the bloody blanket. The body would come up, floating, the hair swirling in the water of the canal under bright noon sunlight.

I turned the light on and sat there, smoking.

Miraglia would be questioning her now.

I got out of bed and started walking. I stood over the telephone and stared at it. If it rang, I would die.

Back in bed with pad and pencil, I listed everything, and tried to find mistakes we'd made, tried to figure where we'd really gone wrong. Finally I stopped that.

Shirley would be the first person questioned when Mayda Lamphier's disappearance came to light.

I had to stop. They'd come and find me babbling.

"Him?" they'd say. "Oh, that was Jack Ruxton. Yeah, too bad. Used to run a TV and radio store. Yeah. Flipped his wig over a screwy teenage broad."

I'll get mine, I thought. I'll get mine.

The money. That's all that counted, all that meant anything. Money was something you could depend on. It was substantial, if you had enough of it. I would have enough. That money was what could keep me sane. The money could perform miracles.

All I had to do was get my hands on it.

That's all.

Then I could forget.

The phone rang. I leaped at it.

"Jack?" she said. "Everything's all right. I knew you'd want to know."

For a second I couldn't speak with the relief.

I said, "Where you calling from?"

"A place, on the way home. It's all right. It's a public phone booth, and there's nobody around."

"Are you all right?"

"I think so."

"What the hell do you mean by that? You think so? If something's wrong, for God's sake, tell me."

"Jack?"

"What?"

"Do you love me?"

"Certainly, I love you. You know I love you."

She hesitated. "Then everything's all right."

My hand was sweating on the phone. I changed hands, and bit my teeth together hard. A goddamned cryptic woman. There was nothing in the world like a cryptic woman. My voice was hoarse. "Shirley?"

"I told you, everything's all right. What more can I say?"

"Tell me what happened."

"Nothing happened, Jack."

"Did it go over? Did you tell your story all right?"

"Of course."

"Well, *what happened?*"

"You don't have to shout, Jack. I can hear you."

"I'm not shouting. I just want to know."

"Well, Doctor Miraglia came in. He acted kind of put out—mad at himself, something like that. I mean, I think it was because he hated losing a patient. Victor in particular. He told me he'd been afraid something like this might happen."

"How did he say that?"

"What do you mean?"

"I mean, did he act suspicious?"

"No. Not that I could tell. Why should he?"

"Forget it."

She said, "He seemed terribly concerned over Victor dying, though. I mean, he acted really sorry. It seemed to hit him awfully hard—I mean, for a doctor. After all, doctors see a lot of that sort of thing."

"Shirley. Exactly how do you mean? How did he act? What did he say? This is important, I think."

"Well, I can't say any more than I have. I told him the intercom system apparently wasn't working. I said I was outside, and everything, just as we planned. So I must have missed hearing him call. I put on a— pretty good act. I think."

"You didn't overdo it."

"No. I was careful. They took Victor away in the ambulance. Then Doctor Miraglia tried out the intercom, and agreed that was how it must have happened. He told me I mustn't feel bad about it."

"You're trying to say something, Shirley. Goddamn it. Say it, whatever it is. Let it come out."

"I'm scared."

"Well, so am I. You don't go around doing what we did every day in the week. You've got to stop being scared."

"It's not so much Victor. It's Mayda."

For a bright moment, in my mind's eye, I saw Shirley ramming that carving knife into Mayda Lamphier's back.

"Just don't worry." I said.

"You think I should report her missing, Jack? You think that might be the thing to do?"

"Will you forget her!"

"Yes. All right."

"What else did Miraglia say?"

"To be honest, Jack—he acted as if it were his own father dying. That's exactly how he acted."

"Oh."

"Somebody might come. I'd better go."

"Yeah."

Her voice was pleading. "Say you love me."

I told her I loved her.

"I want to see you so badly," she said.

"Me too," I said. And at that moment I meant it. Alone, I faced the longest night of my life.

Eleven

It was in the papers the next day. Victor Spondell had died of heart failure, brought on by a long-time respiratory ailment. Surviving was his adopted daughter, Miss Shirley Angela. There was a brief summary of his background.

There was nothing about Mayda Lamphier.

Well, I began to know what this business means when they talk about a criminal returning to the scene of the crime. It was one hell of a pull. I wanted to go out there to the canal, and just see if everything was all right. Just stand there and stare at the spot where the car was, and where she was. Just to reassure myself.

I didn't go. But that pull was hard.

I wanted to see Shirley plenty bad. I didn't like the way she'd sounded over the phone. I couldn't call her, I couldn't go near her place. I had to wait.

I knew it was too early for her to start checking on the money. Or, was it? How did an innocent person act? Would they go right down to the bank and put in their claim for the money? Or would they wait for what they call a "proper" length of time?

It was all I thought about. In the midst of the turmoil, it was the money that was bright and shining.

I didn't hang around the store much that day. I couldn't think right. I kept having the urge to go up to somebody and say, "Well, for gosh sakes, look here. That Victor Spondell kicked off. What you think of that?"

Nobody mentioned his dying. Naturally. Who was Victor Spondell to them? He was nothing. But just let it come out *how* he died, and the whole town would shake itself apart.

Shirley didn't call. I went home and sat by the phone, but there was no word about anything. I didn't sleep. I just lay there in bed with the light on and stared at the ceiling, smoking one cigarette after the other.

I tried to think of Rio, but even that wasn't any good anymore. Nothing was any good.

There was no word for two days. Then, in the morning paper:

MYSTERIOUS DEATH OF WOMAN
Canal Holds Tragic Secret

Tangled about the steering post and wheel of a sporty convertible, a young woman died last night, trapped under the murky waters of the old Blackland Canal, one mile east of this city. Authorities are concerned over the discovery by two fishermen of the as yet unidentified body. The car was a convertible Pontiac of late vintage, registered under the name Henry C. Lamphier, this city. Mr.

*Lamphier will be located. Anyone having a clue as
to the possible identification of the woman should
immediately telephone Police Headquarters, the
Sheriff's Department, or the Florida State Highway
Patrol.*

*Since this newspaper was going to press when
the item was disclosed, it is possible that by the
time you read this, the body will have been identi-
fied through the automobile's registration.*

*Two fishermen (both names withheld by request)
were spearing along the mossy banks of the cen-
tury-old canal late last night, in a skiff, when they
made the somewhat macabre discovery. One said,
"The less I am reminded of this, the better. It was a
terrible thing. I never want to go spearing again."
Police are concerned over the manner in which the
woman's body was entangled with the car. They
believe there is the possibility of foul play. Taking
into consideration the fact that....*

I didn't exactly stop reading. My hands crumpled
the paper into a wad, then shredded it, and for some
reason all I could see in my mind was Shirley taunting
Victor Spondell, as he died. I knew it was only a
question of time before they knew who the "unidentified woman" was. They probably knew now.

Shirley, standing over Victor Spondell, laughing at
him, because I knew she had felt nothing over his
death. Not really. It had been removal of pain, of

fierce pain, and inside her was nothing but angry composure over his death.

Mayda was another thing. They would go to her, question her. I didn't know what to do. But I began to know that she had to get to the bank, and get her hands on that money. At the same time I realized, as I'd thought before, that it might not look right, taking any of it so soon. If things went right, then we wouldn't have to go near that money.

If.

What an unholy word.

Somehow I had to get hold of myself. Now was the time when being calm counted. There was no real reason to fly apart. Nobody had accused Shirley or me of anything. There was no reason even to cast a suspicious glance our way, if you looked at it the way the law would look at it.

An old man who had been on the tricky edge of death for a long time had finally died. At the same time, a woman had died in a car accident. They would backtrack and there would be the gas station attendant to verify the fact that she had been driving while drunk.

So would they find alcohol in her blood, if they performed an autopsy? I didn't know. In all probability, Mayda Lamphier had been drinking to some extent before she came over and slammed into Shirley. Only she hadn't been drinking much. Maybe it would be enough.

I went into the living room, still holding the wadded

newspaper in my hand. It was late morning. I hadn't slept. I felt like hell. I had to see her, talk with her, and I could think of no way. If I tried calling her, there was every chance somebody might be there, questioning her about Mayda.

The buzzer sounded.

I just stood there, staring at the door. The apartment seemed unduly quiet. I realized I was still holding the newspaper.

The buzzer sounded again. There was something lazy, and very patient about the sound of the buzzer.

I went over to my desk, tossed the crumpled newspaper into the wastepaper basket, then walked to the door and opened it.

It was Doctor Miraglia.

"Hi," he said.

He stood there soberly. I tried to grin. It must have looked great, because a nerve was jumping in my face.

"I stopped around at your store," he said. "But they told me you were, sleeping late these days."

"Been hitting it hard," I said. "Come on in, doctor."

"Thanks."

He stepped inside and I closed the door. He wore a suit today, a pale blue gabardine. A pale yellow shirt, the collar open, and without a tie. He was very calm as he turned to look at me, the rimless glasses glinting faintly against the smooth pink coloring of his flesh.

"You go right ahead with whatever you were doing,"

he said in that mild voice. "I just wanted to talk with you for a few minutes. If you could spare the time."

Miraglia was a man who would carefully finish his sentences.

"Sit down," I told him. "Just getting ready to head for the store. But I'm in no hurry. That place is running me ragged lately."

"I'll bet."

He went over and sat down on the couch in front of the windows at the front of the apartment. He looked extremely clean, and not a hair of his black mop was out of place. I came over and took a chair across from the couch.

The silence of the apartment was even more pronounced.

He sat there. He shook his head mildly.

He said, "I suppose you know why I'm here?"

"Can't say that I do."

He didn't speak for a minute. He would come to the point in his own good time. And when I looked at him, all I could see were the bright opaque circles of the lenses of his glasses where they caught the light from across the room.

"Well," he said. "You must have read about it in the papers."

"I'll bet you mean Spondell. That old guy?"

"Yes," he said. "That's who I mean."

"I read about it, the other day. Died." I leaned forward. "Doc," I said. "I couldn't figure why all the bother about that stuff they had me put in the house. Frankly, he looked pretty bad to me. I figured it would be a short time."

"Yes."

I leaned back. I had taken the wrong tack. I was so nervous it was all I could do to keep from jumping up and pacing the room. I had to sit here and talk with him, just as long as he felt like talking.

I put one elbow on the chair arm, and pointed a finger at Miraglia. Sometimes you could put them on the defensive that way, at least I'd done it to customers. "You know?" I said. "I couldn't help but feel sorry for that poor kid—Miss Angela. It must have been rough on her."

"His dying?"

"No. Taking care of him. I mean, young as she is, she should be out with kids her own age."

"It was rough."

I was blabbering. I should be sitting here listening to him tell me why he was here, not telling him things.

He faintly cleared his throat, looked around the room, then focused those damned lenses on me again. I wished I could see his eyes.

"I was rather attached to Victor," Miraglia said. "He was just a patient, but sometimes patients become good friends. It was that way in this case. He was an arrogant old fool, who didn't really believe he would die. I liked him."

He paused and I didn't speak.

He said, "Victor shouldn't have died, Mr. Ruxton."

"Shouldn't have died?"

"He wasn't due. Not really." He shrugged, then said, "Of course, he did die. I even suppose I was afraid he might die. But it wasn't entirely natural, his dying. It was really an accident, beyond his control."

"How's that?"

He didn't speak for a moment. He sat there, rubbed the side of his jaw with the heel of his hand, and shook his head.

"That intercom system," he said. "It went on the blink. Shirley was outside the house when it all happened. She didn't hear him call. A terrible thing—what must have gone on in that bedroom."

I made a deep frown and held it. Here it was. "You must be mistaken," I said. "That intercom system was working fine."

"Now, look, Mr. Ruxton. Don't get on the defensive. I'm not accusing you of anything."

Everything would have been all right, maybe, if he hadn't used that word. "Accusing." He was a corker, quick to work his psychological gimmicks. I hadn't had a chance to be on the defensive.

"I don't get you," I said. "I don't get you at all."

"I think you do."

"I don't."

"Nobody else is here, Mr. Ruxton." He reassured himself of that by glancing quickly around the room. "Just you and me. It doesn't matter what you tell me. We both know how a careless soldering job can ground out a circuit if it's in an especially vital part, don't we? And since you're in the business, you must have realized that you made an extremely inadequate job of soldering that condenser that went out."

I waited a second to make it look good. "So, that's it," I said.

"That's it. I checked the units myself. I located the spot. I used to fool around with electronics myself. It interests me." He lifted one hand and motioned with it, then laid it carefully on the couch beside him, as if it were a piece of fragile glassware. "It was an accident, of course—in a manner of speaking."

"What are you getting at?"

"You knew that was a sloppy soldering job, didn't you?"

"It worked. I don't have time to…"

He interrupted brightly. "You don't have time." His voice became mild again. "It's a shame you don't have time, Ruxton. If you'd had time, that 'old guy' would have been alive right now."

"Boy, you're hot, you are."

"I said I'm not accusing you of anything. It's just the way it is, and I wanted you to know I knew."

"All right. So we both know."

"And nobody else knows. There's certainly no need for them knowing, is there."

I didn't say anything at all to that. I wanted to get up and throw him out on his ear. I couldn't do that, either. He had me so far up a tree I couldn't see the ground for the branches.

On the other hand, it was out, and I had expected this. It had worked all right. Miraglia knew why Spondell had died, and he knew it was my fault. The only thing was, I had figured to be sad about it. How could I be sad when he had me so damned irked I could wring his throat? And something else I didn't like was his too obvious deep concern over the thing.

"All right," I said. "If you look at it that way, I guess maybe it was my fault."

"Sorry I had to bring the news."

"Then why did you bring it? Just to cheer up my day?"

He said, "I want you to know I thought an awful lot of Victor. We had become very good friends. I even had a notion I might be able to get him back on his feet. I couldn't clear him up entirely, but I could have maybe added a couple more years to his life. That's why I've come to you, to tell you what you've done."

"Seems to me you're kind of over-ready to blame somebody."

"I told you, I thought a lot of him."

"You said all that. What's the matter? He leave you part of his loot? That it? I'd think you'd be happier with him gone, if that's the case."

He didn't speak. Right away I wished I hadn't said that. The glasses gleamed and glinted, and his face had paled.

"I'm sorry," I said. "I'm sorry I said that. It just jumped out. I didn't mean it. Guess I'm taking it out on myself. I feel bad about what's happened, what you've told me. I see now, it was my fault—in a way."

He still said nothing.

I said, "The fact is, I kind of liked the old guy myself. He always called me a son of a bitch."

Miraglia didn't change expression and he did not speak.

"Well," I said. "There's nothing anybody can do now."

He grunted softly, as if he'd been punched.

I said, "At least the girl, there—she'll be well taken care of, now. She won't have anything to worry about. She can go off somewhere and have herself a rest. She sure must deserve it."

"How do you mean 'well taken care of'?" Miraglia said.

"Don't tell me Spondell wasn't loaded. It's pretty obvious who he'd leave it all to."

"Is it?"

I frowned at him.

"You're right," he said. "Victor did leave Shirley some money. A lot of money."

"Okay, then."

I was trying to act as natural as possible, and say the things any disinterested party might say.

"Only," he said. "It'll be at least a year before she can touch any of the money."

It was like being struck across the face, hard. My jaw started to drop. I said, "Oh?" fast. It came out as a kind of croak, but I let it go. "How do you mean?" I said.

I was numb all over. It made me dizzy, just sitting there looking at him. Every muscle in my body was like a steel strap, and I was trying hard to recover balance.

"It's rather involved," Miraglia said. "And I'm no lawyer, but I can explain it fairly well. It boils down to the fact that when a person dies intestate, the money goes to the next of kin. Meaning, in this case, Shirley. But," he said. He really laid into that *'But.'* "The next of kin can't touch the money for eight to twelve months. Twelve is the real figure. He can't have any part of it till then. This doesn't leave Shirley in a very comfortable position, as you see. She has no funds of her own. I presume the attorney, or the judge, or the administrator the judge appoints, will work out something for her. Though the law is emphatic." He shrugged, and I sat there sort of tuned in on him as if he were a distant radio station with lots of atmospherics.

"That's tough," I said.

He said, "As for getting the money Victor left her—" He moved his head slowly from side to side. "At least a year. It has to be published. By that I mean in newspapers throughout the country. A formality, in this case. It's done because of the law, to give anyone who might contest a chance to step forward.

This takes time. The law doesn't hurry, Ruxton. It grinds exceeding slow."

By now I had a fair grip on myself. But I was under water all the way. "I'll be darned," I said. "I never knew about that."

I felt dead. Because if we had to run, we would ride the rails, or not go at all.

"All because an intercom didn't work," Miraglia said. " 'For the sake of a nail, the shoe,' and so forth."

"You're riding me," I said. "Come off it."

He looked down, then up at me again. "Maybe it's my turn to be sorry," he said. "I shouldn't ride you like this. I just—I don't know. It troubles me." The glasses glinted. "It just gnaws at me all the time. I've waited ever since he died to say something to you. I had to say something to somebody. I couldn't let it go."

I stood up. "Well, you've sure said it. I feel plenty bad."

He didn't move. He didn't seem to realize I was on my feet, waiting for him to leave. He had something else on his mind. I had to know what it was. The guy was really beginning to scare me. I sat down again.

"I know you're anxious to get to the store," he said, absently. "I suppose you read about Shirley's next door neighbor?"

Somehow, I spoke. "No. I don't believe—what's that?"

He was watching me closely. I sat like a rock. Inside I was flying to pieces.

He tipped his head. "Shirley feels very bad. Everything on top of everything else. Strange you didn't see it—it was on the front page of this morning's paper."

"I haven't read the paper yet."

"You take the paper?"

"Sure—I—"

"Get it."

Already I had remembered balling it up and throwing it in the wastepaper basket. I creaked out of the chair and walked numbly across the room. "I didn't get it in, yet," I said. I realized I was doing everything all wrong. I turned and went back to the chair and sat down. "What's it about, anyway? I'll read it later."

"Mrs. Lamphier. I think you met her, fixed her TV set, or something."

"Oh—her. Sure. I remember her."

"She's dead. They hadn't discovered who she was when the paper went to press. But they know now. She drove into the old Blackland Canal—you know where that is." He didn't say it as a question, but we waited for me to answer.

"No. Don't believe I do."

"No matter. She apparently got drunk and drove into the canal and drowned. Her husband's in Alaska. He's a mining engineer. They've called him home."

"That's sure tough."

"Isn't it?"

"When did it happen?"

"As close as the medical examiner has come, he says probably the same night Victor Spondell died."

"I see. Well—"

Miraglia stood up suddenly. "You know?" he said. "I feel much better now?"

"Glad."

"I had to talk to somebody."

"Know how it is."

"Old Vic, he was kind of like a father to me. Something like that. I thought a lot of him."

"I can see that."

"Yes, well— I won't take up any more of your time, Ruxton. Better be going." He glanced at his watch. "Behind time," he said. "Got the hospital rounds to make yet this morning." He started toward the door. He glanced at the desk. The newspaper was as big as life, sticking up out of the wastepaper basket, balled and crumpled and shredded. I couldn't tell whether he saw it or not. In any event, he couldn't say for sure if it were today's paper.

"I could at least have fixed some coffee," I said.

He didn't reply. He was nearly to the door. I saw his back stiffen. He turned, went over to the desk, stooped above the wastepaper basket and took out the paper.

I stood there. I couldn't speak. I watched him unfold the mess of shredded leaves and look at the front page. Then he crumpled the paper up again and tossed it into the basket. He turned without looking at me and walked toward the door again.

"What was all that for?" I said.

He stopped and looked at me.

He said, "That was today's paper, Ruxton. I thought you said you hadn't seen today's paper."

"Today's? You must be mistaken."

"Yes. Certainly."

I went over to the basket. I took the paper and looked at the date. I shook my head. I frowned. It was all stage acting, and lousy, at that. But I did remember not to make much of a to-do about it.

"The maid," I said. "She was here earlier. I was still in bed. I hardly ever bother reading the paper here. She knows that. She must have thrown it away."

"Maids can play hell," Miraglia said. "Well, I'll be running along. Oh," he said. "You can read that story about Mrs. Lamphier now. If you like. The front page is rather torn up. But I guess you can make it out."

I started for the door. He opened the door and went out and closed it softly behind him.

Twelve

When the door had clicked shut I covered my face with both hands and just stood there. I didn't know whether he was wise to anything. I didn't know. Everything he did and said could all have been strictly on the up and up, completely natural. On the other hand...

I went over and sat down in the chair.

I was perfectly calm now, as calm as I'd ever been in my life. My mind began to function at a steady pace, and everything it read off to me was very bad. I took it all like a punch-drunk fighter, not even bothering to rock with the blows.

I had to talk with Shirley, and I couldn't possibly call her on the phone. There was no way of my going out there now. Only I had to see her.

What a crazy thing to do—saying I hadn't seen the paper. A tiny flaw. Like a mountain.

Nerves? Brass? Miraglia had the stuff. A real honest to God corker. He didn't give a damn about anything. The way he'd turned and gone after that newspaper had been something to see. How many people would do that? And, if they did, why would they? The average guy would let it go. Even if he suspected the paper might be today's paper, he would let it go. Unless he was suspicious.

Why was Miraglia suspicious?

I knew I had to see Shirley.

I came out of the chair and started pacing the floor.

The money. A year. We couldn't wait a year. I couldn't wait a year. I wouldn't.

Wouldn't I? What could I do?

I went into the bedroom, and looked at myself in the minor over the bureau. My face was plenty grim. I was dressed except for my jacket. I grabbed one off a hook in the closet, and got out of there.

I drove to Tampa and got a gun.

Even doing it, I didn't know why I was doing it. I just wanted a gun. Maybe it was just a way to be doing something. A reason to get out of town for a while, and just let the thoughts drift through my head.

I drove around Tampa, looking. I didn't want to try the hockshops, because I knew you'd have to sign a purchase slip. After a while, I spotted a run-down antique store, and went in. I told the old lady in charge that I was just looking around, and she let me be. Finally, I found what I wanted. It was a beat-up old P-38. The old gal was at her desk, poring over a ledger. I moved on around, looking, then passed the gun again, lying among some Arabian knives with slim, curved blades. I checked the old lady. She was looking at the ledger. I slipped the P-38 into my pocket, and picked up one of the knives. It looked the best of them.

"Guess I'll take this," I told her.

I paid for it and got out of there. Three blocks away, I threw the knife down a storm drain.

In the center of town, I stopped at a sporting goods store, and bought a box of 9mm shells. No questions.

I drove home. On the way, I stopped the car on a country road, loaded the P-38, hoping it was a safe job. Some of these automatics would blow apart in your face, because of sabotage in the Nazi factories during the war. But U.S. factory loads were milder than European, and the gun was built for European, so I took the chance.

I fired several rounds out the car window at a bank of dirt. The action was okay.

I drove back to the apartment. I had the gun, but I didn't know exactly why. I put it in the glove compartment of the car, and somehow felt better. It had been a lot of trouble to go through, just to find an old automatic. On the other hand, if I needed it, I had it.

All this time, the business Miraglia had told me about not being able to get the money rode in the back of my mind, blossoming like cancer.

As I reached the door to the apartment, I realized the telephone was ringing. By the time I made it inside to the phone, it had ceased.

I sat there. I didn't move from the phone for over an hour. It didn't ring again. It could have been a lot of people. It might have been Grace. But all I could think was that it had been Shirley, and she'd had to call.

And I hadn't been here to catch the call.

I got out the telephone directory and checked.

Anthony Miraglia. 1414 Emerald Lane. He had offices in the Medical Building, downtown.

I stared at his name until the letters blurred.

Finally, I just sat there and smoked. I didn't go near the store all day. I called in once and told Mrs. Noxton I felt ill, and thought I'd hang around the house. There was nothing of importance, she said, so it was okay.

By the time night folded down, I was a caged tiger.

I took the car and drove over to 1414 Emerald Lane, and checked where he lived. It was a twenty-thousand dollar lay-out, small ranch-type. Completely unpretentious. Some lights were lit, and there was a young kid out front, playing with a red wagon under the porch light. A dog cut out of the shadows by the house and chased the car, yapping his head off.

I snarled at him out the window. He snarled back.

He chased me like a maniac for six blocks, yapping every minute of the way, and every yap was like a spike driven into my gut.

I drove home to sit and smoke some more.

It was a little after nine when the phone rang.

"Jack?"

"Shirley—where are you? I've been nuts."

"Yes. It's all right. I can talk. There's nobody here."

"You shouldn't be talking from the house."

"It's all right. How are you?"

"Terrible. What's with you?"

"Lots."

"Miraglia was here."

"I know."

"How do you know? Did you see him?"

"Yes. He's been around again."

"What did he say?"

"I'll get to it. Have you missed me?"

I started to snap out something. I said, "You know I have."

"I've missed you, awfully. I want to see you so bad, I don't know what to do. In this house. All alone. Can't we…?"

"No. Listen, Shirley. He told me something. He said you can't get the money, that you have to wait a year. I never knew this. It's the law—the waiting. We can't touch the money, Shirley."

"What? Who told you that?"

"Doctor Miraglia."

"He's wrong," she said. "He knows that isn't so. Why, for goodness' sake, the money's already in my name. I went to the bank this morning. I wanted to let you know, but there simply was no way. I didn't dare call before now, so much has happened."

I couldn't speak for a minute. Finally I said, "The money's in your name?"

"Certainly, Jack. Not a bit of trouble. None at all. They expected me in. There was nothing to it. Victor had signed a trust agreement with the bank. I didn't know that. I thought there was a will, or something."

"A trust agreement?"

"Yes. All they did was make out another bankbook, in my name."

I sat there.

"Jack?"

I didn't say anything. I couldn't.

"Are you there, Jack?"

"Yeah. Shirley, Miraglia told me it was the law— that if…"

"He must have been talking about a simple will. That's how that works. Then there's a whole lot of red tape."

"What did you say before, about Miraglia knowing you wouldn't have any trouble?"

"He knew. He knew there was a trust agreement. He told me he'd known, when I saw him after I came home from the bank. He was waiting in the house."

"In the house? When was this?"

"This morning. Maybe ten-thirty. What's the matter?"

Miraglia had come directly from her place to my apartment. He had known she already had the money in her name when he was feeding me the guff about not being able to get the money. I knew—*this was it*.

"Shirley, we've got to make a move. I don't know how much time we have."

"What do you mean?"

"Miraglia's wise, he's wise to something. I don't know what." I explained why I'd said that. "He was here spilling a whole bunch of crap, lying his head off. He was feeling me out. And I goofed plenty. I'm positive of that."

She was silent.

"There's no doubt about it," I said. "If we stick, we don't have a chance. It's only a matter of time. He's looking for something, and when he finds it, he'll light the fuse that will blow us straight to hell."

"I can't believe it," she said. Her voice was flat. "What did we do wrong?"

"You mean what did we do right?"

She spoke loudly. "Stop scaring me, Jack!"

"He's got a bug up," I said. "Believe me."

"Henry's home," she said. "He's with Doctor Miraglia, right now. They went out together. I saw them."

"Henry who?"

"Lamphier. Mayda's husband. He flew in from Alaska. He's all broken up. I talked with him."

"That does it," I said. "We've got to leave town. We can't possibly take a chance and stay." I remembered the money and what time it was. The banks were closed. They opened at nine-thirty the next morning. With my luck, tomorrow would be a bank holiday. I dropped the phone and dove for the newspaper, checking the date. Shirley kept calling to me, her voice crackling over the wire. Tomorrow would have to be all right, we would have to get through the night somehow. I came back to the phone. I felt hollow and scared. I knew if I let go I would just run. "We've got to make it through the night," I said. "You'll pick up the money in the morning and we'll take off."

"Jack, will you please slow down. You're supposed to be the sane one."

"I'm not sane. Not anymore. That was somebody else you knew."

Her voice got tight and frightened. "How do you think it will look, me traipsing into the bank and asking to draw out all that money? Stop being foolish. You can't be right about these things. Doctor Miraglia wouldn't hurt a flea. He feels bad about Victor, that's all. I'm sure…"

"Don't kid yourself. I'm so right about this, I'm bleeding. Just thank your lucky stars we can get hold of that money. Because if it had been another way, we'd be running broke." I stood there holding the phone, with this wild feeling inside me. She didn't say anything. "What have you been doing," I said. "Why didn't you get in touch with me?"

"You said not to. But I would have, if I'd been able. The funeral was yesterday. I've had a million things to do. It hasn't been easy."

The funeral, I'd completely forgotten that there had to be a funeral. It hadn't entered my mind. Victor Spondell had died and vanished and that was that. Shirley must have gone through plenty. She'd been the one who'd had to face everyone.

"Jack?"

"Yeah."

"Running away will only make them all the more suspicious. Don't you see?"

"All the more? Look," I said. "Please believe this. If we stick around, they'll nail us down, and we'll never wriggle out."

"But how? Why should they? How can they prove anything?"

"All they have to do is add things up. This goddamned Miraglia is the one who can add, and he'll add for everybody. They don't need proof. All they have to do is start looking around, asking questions, and putting pieces together. We might have made it if it hadn't been for Mayda. There's no use counting the 'ifs' now. An autopsy will show she wasn't drunk. So, that's count one. Why was she swerving all over the road? The gas station attendant will say he saw the car. They'll find the truck driver I cut in front of. They'll find she wasn't alive when she hit the water.

The wound in her back will be checked. They'll know damned well it wasn't made by a broken support from the convertible top of her car...."

"But you said all of that was perfect."

"It was perfect. But not when somebody's snooping, suspicious and anxious to turn up something."

"Oh, Jack!'

"Yeah. Cripes. Then there'll be the unknown person who saw my truck in front of your place that night. If they ask me about that, I'll have to say I was there on a service call. Maybe somebody saw the truck over by the lake, how do I know?"

I thought of Grace. I wanted to tell her about Grace, but somehow I couldn't bring it out. I should have told her long before this.

I said, "You beginning to catch on, now?"

She didn't speak.

"We're in it," I said. "We've got to run. Running's the only way out."

"It makes us guilty."

"We *are* guilty. Will you get that through your head?"

"We should never have done it."

"But we *did* do it."

Neither of us spoke for a moment. I knew she must feel the same as myself. Lost and sick and trapped.

I said, "I don't have a cent, Shirley. We could run, now—but I'd rather take the chance for the money.

We may never make it. It all depends on what they turn up tonight—how soon they act; whether or not Miraglia goes to the police with what he has. If we left now, we'd never have anything."

"We'd have us, Jack."

"What the hell are we without the money?"

She didn't answer. She sure as hell knew the answer.

Finally, her voice came across the wire. It was soft, and there was something almost sad in it. "All right."

"It just hasn't worked out the way we wanted it to. We could stay and watch them close in, and try to beat them. But we'd never beat them. You know that."

"Yes, Jack," she said. "What do you want me to do?"

"It's still got to look as good as we can make it."

"Don't you think it's bad, talking all this while on the phone?"

"Sure, it's bad. But we can't see each other. You know that!"

"All right."

"Here's what I want you to do. Play it straight. You pack some things tonight. Anything, it doesn't matter what—just to make it look good. Then write a short note to Miraglia. He's the only possible person you'd really have any reason for telling anything. Right?"

"Yes."

"Make it short. You can't stand living where you are any longer. You want to get away. You're going on a vacation, for a month. You'll be back. Never mind where you're going, anything like that. Mail that to him. Write it tonight, and mail it tomorrow—after we get the money."

"Suppose he comes around?"

"Stall him. Don't tell him you're leaving, for God's sake. Just be nice to him. That's all."

"What about Henry Lamphier?"

"Nothing about him. You don't owe him anything."

"Just a wife, that's all."

I ignored that. I was thinking fast, and everything seemed to be working out fine in my mind. "You get to the bank the first thing in the morning. Let's say, quarter to ten. It opens at nine-thirty. Ask for two hundred thousand, cash."

"But, Jack!"

"Not a bank draft. It's got to be cash. You'll have to take a small overnight case, or a small suitcase— something, because it'll be quite a wad. Now, I know it's a hell of a thing. But you've got to get bills of small enough denominations so we won't be stuck with any of them."

"But, Jack—"

"We can't take a chance on a bank draft. This is the one chance we've got to take. They'll frown on releasing that much dough. But they'll have to give it to you. If they pry—and they might—make some remark about having a good investment, if you feel you can bring it off right. They'll say something, as sure as hell. But they've got to give you that money as long as it's in your name. You figure you can't say anything that'll sound right, don't say anything. Just give them the fish eye."

"Why not take all the money?"

"How much is there?" I heard the catch in my voice.

"In cash, there's three hundred, forty-six thousand dollars, and seventeen cents. Exactly. There's more in…"

"Never mind. We can't." I swallowed hard. "It's too much of a risk. They'd still have to give it to you, but they might pull something screwy." I paused a minute. "Christ," I said. *"Three hundred thousand."*

"It's just money," she said.

"Yeah. Well, I don't like the idea of taking it all. It makes me wary. It's bad enough the way it is."

"I can't see why," she said.

I ignored her again. "Then we'll take off," I said. "I'll work the rest of it out. We'll have to get rid of my car and get another. You take a taxi downtown."

"Then what?"

"Wait a minute." I tried to think, I was confused. All I could think of was that money. I could see it in my mind's eye, as clear as anything. I could actually see the bills themselves, in neat, crisp bundles. Stacked together. I couldn't concentrate on anything else. It was crazy.

"Jack? What should I do then?"

"All right," I said. "You do this. You leave the bank, and take the alley beside the bank. Walk through to First Avenue North. Turn East, and walk to the corner of Seventh Street. Got that?"

"Yes, sure. Alley—down First to Seventh. All right."

"I'll be there. Don't look for my car. I'll have a different car, by then. I'll be parked in front of the drugstore on the corner. If I'm not there, you wait in front of the drugstore."

"Where will we go?"

"We aren't going anywhere, Shirley. Not for a long time. I'll tell you about that tomorrow. I'm working something out."

"But, Jack."

"It's all right, I tell you. All we've got to do is have enough luck to get through to maybe ten o'clock tomorrow morning."

"Jack, I've been watching out the window. I've got the house lights off. A car keeps going up and down the street. I know it's the same car, because it's yellow—a yellow hardtop. It keeps going up and down."

Grace. As sure as hell. I would have to tell Shirley about Grace, but I couldn't bring myself to do it now.

"It's nothing," I said.

"I want to see you," she said.

"In the morning."

"I want to see you so bad, I can't think. I'm in love with you, remember?"

"Yeah, honey—buck up, now."

"I'd better hang up, you mean. Harry Lamphier just turned in his drive. He's parking. Doctor Miraglia isn't with him, now."

"Then, with luck, we've got tonight."

"What?"

"They aren't going to do anything yet tonight. They haven't found what they're after. It's going to take them a little time. Maybe they haven't gone to the cops yet. Everything's circumstantial. It can burn us, but they don't have any real proof yet. So they won't move in. I've been trying to figure anything solid they could base suspicions on. It's close, because if it's turned over to the law, they can make an arrest on suspicion alone. But we're still all right, I think."

"I'd better hang up. Let's not take chances."

"You got everything straight?"

"Yes. Jack—he's coming over here."

"Okay. I'm with you. Chin up."

"Here comes that yellow car again."

Thirteen

Doom. You recognize Doom easily. It's a feeling and a taste, and it's black, and it's very heavy. It comes down over your head, and wraps tentacles around you, and sinks long dirty fingernails into your heart. It has a stink like burning garbage. Doom.

I sat up all night with the lights on. Waiting.

At seven-thirty in the morning, I was in Tampa again, making a trade for another car. I had to write a check, and I had to use my name. But it would slow them down a fraction, if they moved today, and that fraction was all I needed. It was an oxidized gray Ford sedan, hundreds of which were on the highways.

I was blocks away before I remembered the gun I'd left in the glove compartment of the other car. I had to have the gun; the same old obsession. I drove back, told the guy on the used car lot I'd forgotten some things in the car.

"Okay," he said.

The glove compartment was empty. I went over to him. He was a beer-eyed, seedy-looking bird, wearing a suit that had been pressed with the dirt in it.

"Bet I know what you're after," he said.

"Then hand it over."

"Uh-uh."

"How come?"

"I bought your car. It was a deal, right?"

"But for cripes' sake. I left some personal stuff in the car. That certainly doesn't go with the deal."

"Make me see it your way."

"It's a shame this is a busy street."

"Isn't it?"

"How much?"

"Twenty bucks."

"You're a real son of a bitch."

"All how you look at it. Twenty bucks is twenty bucks."

By now there was nothing to do but pay him and take the gun. I should never have come back. I should never have gone to him when I found the gun missing. I should have let it go. On the other hand, if I let it go now, he would crow all the more. I paid him and took the gun and left the place. I put the gun and the box of ammunition in the glove compartment of theFord.

I drove back home, trying to keep from thinking. I was so scared I could hardly drive.

It was nine-thirty when I turned into the alley behind the apartment building. Cutting it almost too close. But I had to pick up some clothes I'd packed in a bag, and phone Mrs. Noxton at the store. That would be ticklish, and I wished I hadn't put it off until now. I kept looking at my watch, checking the time, thinking: What's she doing? Did she make it all right downtown, alone, without being seen? Is anybody there with her? Will she be able to get away? Will she lose her nerve?

And I kept trying not to think something else that had occurred to me during the night. It kept coming back to me, hitting harder every time. What was Miraglia's real interest? I couldn't believe he was playing beagle just out of fondness for Victor Spondell. There had to be something else. Had he figured to latch onto some of the money, too? Then something struck me.

Suppose Shirley and Miraglia were together on something, trying to screw me? Set me up for a patsy. Sure. It was crazy thinking. But you think that way just the same, because you don't really know. You never know till you've got that money in your hands.

I parked the car by the garage in the alley, and walked on around to the rear entrance. Inside, a hall led straight on through to the front entrance, and Miraglia was holding the door open for a cop.

"Since his car's not in the garage," Miraglia said, "He's not here." His glasses glinted and gleamed as he talked mildly. The uniformed cop said nothing. Miraglia said, "Let's go on up, all right?"

Two men in plain clothes came in the front door behind the harness cop. I was in shadow behind the stair alcove. Miraglia said something I didn't quite catch.

One of the men in plain clothes said, "Well, we've got a warrant, anyway."

The other man chuckled.

I didn't wait for anything else.

Coming out of the other end of the alley, I drove past on the street bisecting my street, and looked down toward the apartment house. Two police cruisers were parked out front. It had been that close. I could hardly breathe. Another harness bull stood outside by the cruisers.

I kept going.

I drove downtown somehow, without smashing into anybody, and parked across the street from the bank. On the way down, I thought I'd glimpsed Grace's car, and I remembered what Shirley'd said last night, seeing a yellow car running up and down her street.

This was it. They were on it, and we were running behind time.

Maybe they already had Shirley.

It was ten to ten. I had missed Shirley going into the bank. If she had gone into the bank.

I was numb all over. They were in my apartment now. Then I remembered something, and it was as if the world tipped on its axis and sent me spinning off into black space. I remembered making lists of things, on paper, with a pencil, adding everything up to find a flaw.

I remembered doing this twice.

I remembered flushing the paper down the toilet once. What had I done with the other paper?

I forced myself to stay calm. I lit a cigarette and fidgeted. Men and women filed in and out of the brass-trimmed glass bank doors. A uniformed guard lounged outside, looking up at the sky, scratched his chin, then went inside again. Traffic clogged the street. I was so damned worried I began talking to myself. It shouldn't take her this long, if she was in there.

All sorts of crazy things came to mind. Among them was the picture in my mind of a faceless man named Henry Lamphier, disturbed over the loss of his wife. He should be happy. They never were though. Another five minutes and I would have to go inside the bank and check. Then I saw her.

She came out of the bank. She wore an aqua dress, and she looked terrific. It really packed a wallop, how I hadn't seen her in days. She filled that dress. Her auburn hair shone in the bright sunlight. The pallor of her face was somehow strange in this bronzed country. She belonged in a bedroom, naked, on a bed.

I had to get going. I thought of signaling her, but suddenly I couldn't see anything except the bag she carried. I knew what was in that bag. It was shiny white leather. A rectangular-shaped small suitcase, with brass clasps. And all the feeling I'd had at seeing her suddenly changed and focused on that bag.

She didn't spot me.

I flung open the door and waved. I called her name, but not loudly. I couldn't shout at her. It would only draw attention. I got back under the wheel.

She turned and walked down the street along the front of the bank. When she reached the alley, she hesitated again. She changed hands with the bag, looked up and down the street. Abruptly, she turned down the alley, and even from across the street, through traffic, I heard the sharp *clack-clack-clack* of her heels, echoing.

I drove down the street to Seventh, turned left over toward First, and parked at the curb by the drugstore. Looking up along the sidewalk, I saw her come out of the alley and start down toward me. By now, I was soaking with sweat. I wanted to leap out of the car and run up the street to her.

We didn't have time for anything. The only break was the law didn't know what car I was driving. As if that would matter, unless we got out of here fast.

I watched her slim legs scissor along toward me.

"Jack?"

I snapped around in the seat. It was Grace. She had on a thin white sweater, with nothing underneath, and tight black shorts. She was big-bodied and her thighs plumped out under the tight rims of the shorts.

"Jack? What are you doing?"

She was on the sidewalk at the opposite side of the car. She opened the door and slid in across the seat and slammed the door. She pushed up close to me, her leg pressed against me, watching me.

"Grace—get out."

"No."

"I'll throw you out."

"What's the matter with you?"

I looked up the street. Shirley had seen me. She'd seen Grace get into the car as sure as hell. She had slowed her stride and I saw the frown on her face.

"Jack, you're acting awfully damned funny."

"Get out."

I didn't know what to do.

"I'm not going to get out. I've been following you. I was waiting at your place and I saw you drive in behind the apartments with this car. What are you doing, Jack?"

I said, "You want me to wring your stupid neck?"

She put one hand over her mouth. "Jack," she said. "Were those policemen looking for you? Were they? I saw some policemen going inside."

I smelled the gin. This early in the morning and all full of gin.

I looked back up the street. Shirley was crossing

the street toward the car. She hesitated halfway across, looking at me, with her face pinched up.

"Who's that?" Grace said.

Shirley did an about-face, and started back up the street. She really swung it hard. *Clack-clack-clack*.

"Shirley!" I called.

She stopped.

"Shirley—*come on*."

She turned and started walking back toward the car. I had my eyes on that bag in her hand. My stomach was tight up, and aching with tension. I whirled and caught hold of Grace with both hands, and sank my fingers in, and shoved my face up close to hers.

"I'll kill you, Grace, I swear it—I'll kill you if you don't get out—now!"

She saw something in my face.

She began to cry. Her face pudged up and she burst into tears, with her mouth wailing. Just like her. She got out of the car like lightning and slammed the door.

"Jack?" Shirley said from my side. Like ice.

Her face had that look women get. Like you're dead a long time and smell pretty bad, and they want to make sure they don't step on you.

"Come around and get in," I said.

She started around the front of the car.

"Who the hell are *you*, darling?" Grace said to her.

She stood there spraddle-legged, with her breasts stuck out, bawling.

Shirley tried to get past her. I reached over and flung the goddamned door open. Shirley started for the door.

"No, you don't!" Grace said, and grabbed for Shirley.

People were stopping on the sidewalk.

Shirley turned and looked at Grace. Grace said something I didn't get, but from the expression on a woman pedestrian's face, I could tell it was something real filthy.

Shirley hit her smack in the face with the white bag.

It was all I needed. Two dames fighting. At a time like this. I slid across the seat. "Get in, Shirley!"

Grace came at her, claws out. Shirley turned and jumped into the car. I started the engine and took off. Grace was standing back there on the street, yelling bloody murder. She started running after the car, then stopped, right in the middle of the street. Horns blared.

I kept watching in the rear-view mirror. Grace turned and ran to the sidewalk, and off in the opposite direction.

We drove along. "Who was that?"

"Nobody. Forget it. A nutty girl I knew once."

I looked at her. She was sitting very straight and prim, with her skirt pulled down over her knees, knees together, looking out of the windshield. The white leather bag was between us on the seat, I let my hand touch it and the back of my neck got cold.

"Everything go all right?" I said.

I didn't want to scare her yet. She didn't say anything.

I turned and said, "She's a damned fool woman who refuses to leave me alone." My voice rose. "She just happened along on the street. I couldn't get rid of her." I began to shout. "Good Christ, Shirley. I didn't want her around, I knew her once a long time ago. Long before I met you. She won't let me be!"

My ears rang. She didn't say a word.

"Shirley," I said, keeping it down. "I'm sorry she was there. I couldn't help it. I did everything I could to get rid of her."

"That is not what I meant," Shirley said.

We drove along. She didn't speak.

"Shirley, for Christ's sake. Shirley?"

She said nothing.

I wanted to stop the car and tear open the shiny white leather bag and look at what was inside.

"Shirley?"

Nothing.

"Did it go all right, Shirley?"

She just sat there.

I slowed down and tried to drive very carefully. "Shirley?" I said. "It's like this." So I told her all about Grace; everything about her. It was something I should have done at the beginning, and let that be a lesson to me. I laid it on the line and dropped it in her lap. "She's screwy. There was nothing I could do. What would you have me do?"

She had nothing to say. I stopped the car and turned to look at her.

"Shirley." My voice was tight. "Did you or did you not get the money?"

"What if I didn't?"

"Did you get it!"

She didn't look at me. I grabbed the bag and started opening it. The clamps were stuck. I tore at them.

"There's a key," she said.

"Where is it?"

"I have it."

"Well, give it to me!"

"Here." She fished around in a small blue purse, and handed me a flat metal key. My hands were soaking wet and shaking. I couldn't get it in the lock, then I did, and the bag popped open and money tumbled all over the seat between us. It was stacked neatly and it was all in paper-banded packets.

"Jesus H. Christ."

She didn't say anything.

"You made it," I said, staring at the money.

"Yes. That's obvious, isn't it."

"How much?"

"All of it. Three hundred and forty…"

"I told you not to take all of it!"

"I wanted it all."

I stared at her. Well, what the hell did it matter now? She looked at me that way and said, "Was she nice in bed, Jack?"

"Who?"

"That girl? Was she hot? A good lay? Did she really love it up?"

"Cut it out."

"I'm merely asking. I'm serious. She looked as if she could really bounce a bed."

"Shirley, cut it out!"

"Don't shout, darling. People will hear you. It's embarrassing. It may not be to you, but it is to me."

She turned and looked at the windshield.

I packed the money lovingly back into the shiny white leather bag, and snapped the lid shut.

All three hundred thousand dollars of it.

The key was in my hand. Make a gesture, I thought. Go ahead. I looked at the key. It was a hard thing to do.

"Here," I said. "You keep this."

She took the key daintily, without a word, and put it in her purse, and faced front. I reached out and touched her arm. It was like touching a stovepipe.

"Shirley," I said. "Honey. Please. Don't—"

She watched the windshield.

I started the car and drove away, then remembered.

"Where are your bags?"

"At the Greyhound bus terminal. I checked them. I couldn't possibly carry everything."

"We'll pick them up."

I drove over there. She gave me the check. I felt frightened to leave her in the car alone with the money. What else could I do? Carry it with me? I went on in and got her bags, four of them, and put them in the back seat of the Ford. She hadn't moved a muscle. We drove away.

"I didn't think you went for blondes," she said. "I thought brunettes were your dish."

"Cut it out, Shirley."

"Did she like to do it with her clothes on or off?"

"Stop it."

Her tone was flat. "You treated her awfully, Jack, really, you did. She was crying. She must have felt very bad. Is that any way to treat a girl?"

I clamped my lips tight.

"Jack."

I gripped the steering wheel, thinking about those cops back at the apartment.

"Was she as good as I am?" When I didn't answer, she said, "I really want to know, Jack. Honestly. Tell me, just between us—was she better?"

I gnawed the inside of my cheek.

"I suppose we all have our points," she said, "You called her Grace. Grace is such a nice name. It has a certain fillip to it, don't you think? I mean, it's—well, bold, you might say, but not too bold. There's a certain feeling of mystery—"

"Please, Shirley. You've ragged me enough."

"It's just that I'm interested. It's a wonder you never mentioned her to me. She has a beautiful body. She didn't wear falsies, either. Of course, neither do I. But hers were a little bigger, I think. But, then."

I waited. She didn't speak for a moment. I drove toward the outskirts of town. I had wanted everything to run smoothly between us. It wasn't going to be that way. I didn't know how to tell her we were really running now because we had to run.

Only I had the money.

I'd thought "I"—not *we.*

She said something. Then she said, "Oh, darling." Then she said, "Please…" It came out as a kind of sob. She moved across the seat and I slowed the car, wondering, What now?

She shoved the white bag on the floor and put her arms around me.

"I believe you," she said. "I believe you."

She kissed the side of my face, with her arms around my neck, purring to herself the way she did, and half-kneeling on the seat. "Don't you see how it was?" she said. "I just couldn't stand it. That's all. I love you, Jack—I love you." She kissed me on the mouth, and hugged me some more. "I couldn't stand it. I love you so much—so much."

I got a look at her eyes and they were mad for

a second. I mean *mad*, not angry. Then that went away.

"I believed you right away," she said. "But the thought of sharing you with something like that—with *anyone*—it would be too much."

"You never shared me."

"I know, Jack. I'm sorry. Can't you see?"

"I guess."

"Don't try to make me feel worse, now."

"I'm not."

"I wanted to hurt you—to make you feel as bad as I felt." She leaned in tightly against me, kissing me, and purring. I nearly drove the car off the street. "All right, now?" she said. There was something husky in her tone.

"Yeah. I couldn't do anything with her, Shirley."

"I understand."

"We can talk sensibly now?"

"Yes." She knelt there on the seat with her arms around me, her eyes shining. Her hair was tumbled down around one side of her face. "You're my man," she said. "And I love you."

I patted her thigh.

"I got the money without any trouble at all," she said. "Isn't it really better getting it all, instead of leaving some behind? We'll never come back for it. Don't you see?"

"It was the chance itself," I said. "I wasn't sure you could bring it off. It doesn't matter now."

She sank back on the seat, watching me, smiling with a kind of secretiveness. She looked a million. Ten million. I felt really good all of a sudden.

"Shirley?"

"Yes?"

I told her about Miraglia and the police at my apartment, and how we had to run for sure, now. How there was no other way out.

Fourteen

She said a lot of things, and carried on some, but I finally got her calmed down. She was scared. But so was I.

What scared me was the thought of losing that money.

Boiled down, nothing else mattered. That much money was worth being scared about, and it was worth taking chances for. I could have spent my whole life in the store and never managed to gouge even a small part of what we had out of sales.

"You knew this all the time, and you let me act like I did," she said. "I'm sorry, Jack."

She really meant it.

"Listen," I said. "We're not going to have time to talk now. First off, it'll take them a little time to find out about this car...."

"That girl saw it."

"I know, I know. Don't you think I realize that? It can't be helped. I was planning to trade it off for still another. We can't do it, now. If we steal one, that won't help."

"What will we do? Where will we go?"

"Easy, now. Keep hold of yourself. There's only us, you know? We can't take a bus, a train, or a plane.

They'll be watching them. They'll sure as hell set up road blocks before long. They've probably already contacted the bank. They're at your place. They're looking for us right now. The one chance we have got is this car, until they find out about it."

"Yes, Jack."

I headed across town toward the junkyard district.

"They'll have the license number before the day's out. But there are a lot of cars exactly like this one on the highways, everywhere. I'm going to swipe a plate off a wrecked car in a junkyard, then we'll scram."

"Where?"

"Not far. We'll take back roads, head north maybe fifty or seventy miles, and rent a place. Anything. A cabin someplace. Then when everything cools down, we'll take off. The big mistake would be to try and make it now. We'd never make it, Shirley."

She just looked at me.

I made it to a junkyard I knew of, where it was self-service. I parked down the street, told her to lie on the seat, out of sight. Then I went over to the yard, and told the man I was looking for an old Stromberg carburetor to fix up a hot rod I was building for my kid. He said to have a look around.

"I'll need pliers and a screw driver."

He grumbled, and loaned me the tools.

I found a plate for this year, got that off the car it was on, and slid it under my shirt and belt, at my back. Then I located a carb, and tore it off fast.

"You'll need a kit," he said. "This is all shot to hell."

"I know it."

"I sell kits."

"Well, I figured…"

"It's no good without you fix it, pal."

"Okay. I'll take the kit, then."

I paid for the stuff, and went back to the car. She was lying on the seat, looking like a scared rabbit.

I was beginning to feel fine. We had a good chance.

We drove out of town, taking the back routes, and stopped the first chance so I could change the plates. Shirley sat in the car, tuning the radio. She'd been quiet ever since we left town, and that bothered me a little. I buried the plate that was on the car. Then I heard her call.

"Jack. Hurry!"

Well, I went over there, and it was on the radio. She picked up the tail end of a news flash, but even at that, it was pretty explicit.

They were holding Henry Lamphier in a jail cell for his own protection. He had sworn to kill us both. The police were having a bad time with him. We were suspected of murdering both Victor Spondell and Mayda Lamphier, and they had it all straight down the line, even though they claimed they weren't positive. They theorized Mayda Lamphier had some-how surprised us in the act of letting Victor die, and we'd had to do away with her. They uncovered everything. The pad with the list of stuff at my place, Miraglia's name, everybody's name, all the gimmicks. It added up. I don't know, maybe there was something inevitable about it, because they'd even dug up the bloody blanket.

A young cop got credit for that. He had put himself in what he figured was my place, since the Medical Examiner had claimed there would have been a lot of blood, and we had probably wrapped Mayda in something.

He walked away from the spot by the canal, down the road, and turned off where he thought we might have buried whatever it was, and dug up the bloody blanket.

They had checked with the bank at three minutes to ten. So they'd missed Shirley by maybe seconds.

There was nothing on the car as yet.

We were "love killers." We had held "wild orgies" under the very eyes of the pitiful dying man. We were "sex-crazed thieves and lustful murderers." We were "passion-bold." I could see all the fact crime writers streaming toward the house that they called the "love nest death house," and stuff like that.

Behind it all was Anthony Miraglia. He told the police something had made him suspicious. He berated himself for not acting sooner. He had discovered the original condenser I'd taken out of the intercom unit under Victor Spondell's eyes, claiming it was bad. I remembered leaving it on the window-sill. I'd had to take it out with Victor watching.

He had taken the condenser home to his boy, who was interested in building radio kits. Then he looked at it, checked it, and found it flawless. From there on out, one thing had led to another, Doctor Miraglia told them. "Victor Spondell was a strong man, and I admired his courage in view of the fact that he knew he would die. He was my friend."

They said we would never get away.

Something began to go out of me. I had to keep looking at that white bag with the money in it, to reassure myself. It helped.

"It looks bad, Jack."

"Looks and is are two different things," I said. "Keep your chin up, Shirley."

We stopped off in Tampa, got some sandwiches and cokes, and took off.

By late afternoon we had rented a cabin on a river, in the woods. We were "newlyweds." The nearest store and gas station stood at a country intersection about a mile away, called Wilke's Corners.

The cabin was an old place, but pretty well kept up. There were three rooms. A small kitchen, a bed-room, and a living room. The furniture was beat.

The cabin was on a small hill. You could look out the front windows and see the dirt road winding down through pine trees, away from the river. On the other side, you could see the river, and you could hear it, pulsing darkly against the shore. There were cypresses and vines along the river, and the water was black.

We'd had to ask about a place. I asked in a bar attached to the grocery store at Wilke's Corners. A farmer said he had a place, and we rented it sight unseen.

Shirley had waited in the car. But she was still talking about how the man's face looked when I paid him the rent for the first two weeks.

"Well," she said, standing in the living room. "We're here."

"Yeah. It's not bad."

She moved toward me. "It's wonderful, Jack. We're married. We're newlyweds. I like it that way."

"Sure. So do I."

"Kiss me."

I kissed her. I had wanted to bring in the stuff from the car. I didn't get to it right then. I was worried about all they'd said over the radio. I was worried about the guy we'd had to rent the cabin from. I was worried and scared about everything, but nothing seemed to bother Shirley from the moment she entered that cabin door.

She said, "There's nobody here, but us."

"Yeah."

"Nobody to see us, or watch us."

"That's right."

"Just us. All alone. The way it should be."

I held her tightly. It was good this way. You could hear the river and the wind in the pines and it was getting on toward the first part of twilight. Some of the worry fell away from me. The place was warm with our coming. We stood there in the middle of the living room, holding each other, amid the old smells of wood and old fires, and the air was close, but maybe that helped. It was different. There was a kind of freedom in it, and this freedom slowly worked on you, and all the bad fell away.

"We don't have to hurry, or anything," she said. "We can take our time, and do anything we want." She said it in a close whisper, and there was strong excitement behind the words.

I rubbed my hands up and down her body, feeling the shape of her, and pulling her against me. I kissed her lips and her face, and we stood there holding it like that.

She pressed her hands against my chest, and tipped her head up to me, her lips parted, her eyes shining big and round. "Jack." she said. "Do you really know how much I love you?"

I kissed her on the mouth and she moaned softly.

"Jack?" Her eyes had the devil in them now. "Let's just take off all our clothes and be naked together. Not a stitch."

"Hadn't we better get the stuff in from the car?"

I kept thinking of that money out there in the car.

"It can wait." She was already starting to unbutton her dress between her breasts, watching me. She paused. "Are you sorry about anything, Jack? I mean, about what we've done?"

"No."

"Neither am I."

We moved into the bedroom. I yanked the spread back and looked at the bed. It was made up and it looked clean. I saw no bugs or insects in the room. The guy I'd rented the cabin from said he kept it for fishermen mostly, but that it was always ready to be rented to anyone who wanted it.

"Jack?"

"Yeah."

"There's a fireplace in the living room. Why not start a fire, and be real cozy?"

"It's pretty warm for a fire."

"It'll be chilly tonight."

I looked at her and grinned. "I'll bet."

She pouted. "Please. I'd like a fire. We could have a fire, and close all the windows and doors, and be cozy in the firelight."

"Now?"

She breathed it. "Yes. Now. It'll be better. I promise. We don't have to hurry."

I went on outside. I started looking for wood, but somehow I ended up over by the car. I took her bags inside, and then came back and got the shiny white leather suitcase. I got that chill on the back of my

neck again. I took it inside. She was in the bedroom.
I set the suitcase on a chair, and stood there staring
at it.

She came out of the bedroom, carrying a big pile
of blankets.

"You get the wood?"

"I will.

She frowned as she saw me staring at the money
bag.

"Come on, Jack."

I went out. I didn't even ask her what the blankets
were for. I got some wood together, mostly pine, so it
would burn easily, and went back inside again. I was
beginning to feel tired. We were remote from everything, and I couldn't fasten on to what we had done.
We were just here, that's all.

Then I'd think of that money. The chill.

She had the blankets spread all around the floor in
front of the fireplace. I dumped the wood in a box,
and set the fire with some old newspapers underneath the wood. It caught quickly, and the room
became a chimera of fire and shadow. It changed the
cabin. She was right. It was good.

She still had her clothes on, with some of the but-
tons of her dress undone, the round thrust of her
breasts showing.

"We forgot to get anything in to eat."

"There are some cans in the kitchen," she said.
"Not much, but it'll do. Don't you think?"

"Sure."

She moved into my arms, and it started. We didn't get our clothes off right then, either. It was as if she wanted to devour me. I'd never seen anything like it. She was wild. It got me, and we were both swept up in it, a kind of orgy of flesh. And, like always, the pallor of her body seemed to make it stronger somehow. She moaned. She didn't hold back. I saw that she had been holding back the other times. She talked wildly, yelled, and writhed like the flames of hell.

"I won't worry about that Grace anymore," she said once. Then another time, "This! This is for the money. For the money. This!"

It didn't matter. Nothing mattered.

It was dark and the fire had died down to red embers before we rested much. Then we just lay there and she had been right about everything. It was good with the fire. The cabin was warm, and it smelled of her perfume, mingled with burning pine.

"You're a mess," I said.

"You made me that way."

Her aqua dress was all roped up around her middle, and her hair was snarled, and she just lay there, like some glorious whore, glorifying her whoring, happy as hell.

I went over and put some more wood on the fire.

When I turned around, she was naked, lying there on the blankets.

"Get the money, Jack."

I didn't say anything. I turned like a hound on the scent. I got the money bag and brought it back.

"Where's your purse?"

"Over there on the table."

I got the key from her purse and unlocked the white leather bag.

"Pour it out," she said. "Here." She slapped the blanket between us.

I opened the white bag and turned it upside down. The money fell there on the blanket between us, piling up and piling up. I threw the small suitcase across the room, and knelt looking at it.

"It kind of makes you crazy," I said. "Doesn't it?"

"Undress," she said. "Like me. Take your shirt off."

I undressed all the way to make her happy, then we lay there, and looked at the money. The firelight was high now, and the flames danced across the ceiling and played like thin wicked fingers across the pile of money.

"Let's take all the paper bands off," she said. "It'll look like more. Jesus, Jack—just look at it, will you?"

I felt a little crazy, right then. I couldn't help it. Over three hundred thousand dollars, and all mine.

Right there on the floor. I could touch it, and run my hands through it.

"Fun," she said.

"Yeah." My throat was dry.

I looked at her. Her breasts stood out and she sort of sprawled around, stripping the paper bands off packets of the money. There were all denominations. Tens. Twenties. Fifties. Hundreds. There were lots more hundreds than anything else. I helped her. She was a lot steadier than I was. I was sweating to beat the band, stripping those packets.

Then we had this pile of money on the blanket. I couldn't say anything. I knew I would have yelled, or something.

"Just think," she said. "It was all mine. Only now it's ours. I mean, if I hadn't met you, Jack, I'd still be back there feeding Victor his oxygen and secretly burning up inside."

"But it's not that way, so don't think of it."

Shirley knelt by the money. She reached into it with both fists and tossed it into the air, and watched it flutter down.

"Think of all the things we can do," she said.

"I am."

I lay there, watching her. She was beautiful, Christ, they didn't come any more beautiful than Shirley Angela. Kneeling there with that big pile of money, and the firelight playing across her body, breasts, hip and thigh, her flesh sheened a little with perspiration from the heat so it mirrored the flames—there was never anything like it.

She saw the way I looked at her and laughed happily. She stood up, swaying her hips and shoulders in the firelight, then went into a little dance, playing her body against the fire and the shadows.

She came by me and I tripped her. I grabbed her and kissed her and she was hot all over.

"Jack," she said. "I'm so happy. I love you so!"

"Prove it."

She eyed me. "With pleasure!"

We rolled around in that money, loving it up, like a couple of swine, and this time there was nothing slow about anything. It was like that time on the kitchen floor, at her house. Only it was better. It was the best.

After a while, we went into the kitchen, and opened a couple cans of stuff. We ate that, and I made some coffee.

"We'll have to get some groceries," I said.

"How long do you think we'll be here?"

"I don't know." And I didn't, then.

Fifteen

Next day it was the same.

About noon, it was, we packed the money away in the suitcase. We were out of cigarettes, so I said I'd drive over to Wilke's Corners.

"Be careful."

"Don't worry."

I went over and bought groceries, and cigarettes, and two bottles of whisky. Everything went smoothly. I listened to the car radio, but I didn't get anything about us. It was almost too quiet.

When I got back, Shirley had found a radio under the bed and she was listening to it in the living room. She was wearing a red housecoat, and that was all.

"Hi," I said.

She didn't say anything. She didn't look at me.

"Hey, there," I said.

She looked up at me and smiled hesitantly. I went into the kitchen and put the stuff away, and poured a drink.

"You want a drink?" I said.

"No."

I didn't like the way she said that. She was acting strange.

Then she said. "Did it go all right?"

"It went perfect."

"That's good."

"No questions, nothing. I didn't talk to anybody but the grocery clerk, and the guy over at the bar. There was nobody in the bar."

"Oh."

"Something the matter?"

"Oh, no."

I drank the drink. I had another. Then another. I felt it right away, and it felt good, so I had another. I went in and sat down in a chair across from where she was on the couch. She flipped the radio off and looked at me. We watched each other.

"Happy?" she said.

"Sure. You?"

She looked at her lap, then at me, then she nodded.

"Isn't much to do around here," I said.

She turned her head away.

"You know what I mean," I said quickly. "Only we can't take off. It's a shame, in a way. All that dough, and no place to spend it. Wouldn't you like to spend it?"

"Anything you like is all right with me."

"Yeah, but doesn't it stir you up?"

"Not particularly. I've been awfully happy here, Jack."

"Well, I am, too."

We didn't speak for a time.

"You hungry?" I said.

"Not right now."

I was feeling the whisky good. I went into the kitchen and had another.

"Sure you don't want a drink?"

She hesitated. "Maybe just a little one."

I poured her a little one and took it in to her, and watched her sip at it. She watched me over the rim of the glass. I started back to the chair, and my gaze got stuck on that white leather bag with the money in it.

I got that chill.

I turned and went outside.

"Where you going?"

"Be right back."

I went to the car. In the back of my mind there was always that threat, that they knew, and they were trying to find us. I had it all worked out, how as soon as I figured things had cooled down, we'd get out of here, get another car—steal one—and take a plane somewhere. Somewhere in the Southwest, maybe. And from there we would fly to Europe. I'd have to get papers rigged, but I knew I could do that. I could do anything with that money.

Only right now, there was the threat hanging over my head. I opened the glove compartment, and took out the P-38, and the shells. I loaded the gun, and put the shells back in the glove compartment. I took the gun inside and laid it on the mantel over the fireplace. I felt better.

"What's that for? I didn't know you had a gun."

I had a good edge.

"I just feel better with it in here. Bought it the other day. You never know."

"I don't like guns around, Jack."

"Well, it won't bite you."

I went over and stood in front of her. One of her breasts was bare outside the red housecoat. I don't know. We'd been at it and at it, and she was terrific, but there was that money. And the getting away. And the knowing they were out there someplace, looking.

"You're pretty, you know it?" I said.

"Am I?"

"Yeah. There's nobody I'd rather be with."

"Am I really pretty?"

She opened the housecoat and lay back on the couch.

She kept at me and kept at me, all day long. It was like some kind of marathon. And after a while you can wear anything pretty thin. It might have been different if we were in that big hotel down in Rio. But somehow, here, you were always listening. There would be the pulsing of the river, and the sound of the pines, and you would try to listen above that. Straining. Just a little bit.

But she was at me every minute.

Middle of the night.

"Tell me you love me."

I told her a few times. I started to go to sleep,

telling her, mumbling and drifting off. I came awake fast, with a yell. She was kneeling there beside me, beating me with both fists, her face all wrung up, shouting it at me.

"Tell me you love me! Tell me you love me!"

I took her in my arms. "Would I be here if I didn't love you?"

She didn't say anything.

"Jack?"

"Yeah."

"We didn't do anything tonight. We just came to bed."

"Well, for cripes' sake."

"I mean it."

"Okay."

"Jack?"

"Yeah."

She rolled over, with her back to me. "Nothing."

I lay there staring at the dark. You could hear the river pulsing, and the trees moaning. The fire had died down in the other room. There was a lingering acrid odor of stale pine smoke.

"Shirley?"

She didn't say anything.

"Shirley, what was it? What did you want to say?"

"Nothing. I told you. Nothing."

I lay there. She didn't move. Neither did I.

"Come on," I said. "What's the matter?"

She didn't answer.

I thought after a while she went to sleep. I finally slid quietly out of bed and went into the kitchen. I didn't turn on any lights. I got the bottle, and took a long drink. I carried the bottle into the other room, and sat down on the floor, on a blanket, and pulled down the white leather bag. I opened it; looked at the money.

Every time. The same thing.

I took a drink and looked at the money.

I sat there until the bottle was empty. I was drunk as all hell. I sat there staring at the money. I grabbed the bills in my hands and crunched them together in wads. They were crisp.

I got up and staggered over to the fireplace and put a log on the irons. It flamed up. I came back and sat with the money, looking at it, counting it.

I got that crazy feeling again.

Maybe we'd never get away. Maybe we'd be stuck here forever, or maybe they would get us. And we would never have a chance to spend any of it, live the high life, what I had wanted ever since I could remember.

I was really crocked.

Right now, the way things were, with the law alerted, the two of us could never make it.

But maybe I could make it alone.

I looked at the money. I guess that was the first time I had really thought about killing Shirley Angela.

Only I knew I could never kill her.

I just thought about it. How it would be. But I knew I couldn't ever kill anybody. I knew that. Big brave me.

"Jack?"

I looked up. Shirley stood there watching me in the firelight. She was naked. I thought how it would be and knew it was crazy and that I could never do it. She swam around in my vision.

"You're drunk, Jack."

"So what?"

"Well, I'd like a drink, too. You might at least offer me one."

"Okay, okay." I got up and lurched out into the kitchen, found the other bottle of whisky. "Little one?"

"No. A big one."

I poured her half a water glass full, splashed some water on top of it, and took it in to her. I drank another long one out of the bottle. It socked me hard. I sat down with the money. The whole room was going.

I heard a noise and looked up.

"You still here?" I said.

"Yes. I'm still here. Pour me another." She handed me the empty glass.

"Well," I said. "An old toper, eh?"

"No."

I poured her another big one and she took it and

drank it. I looked at the money and heard a crash. I looked up. She had thrown the glass into the fireplace. She stood there grinning at the fireplace.

"Watch it," I said, "You're getting plastered."

She turned and looked at me, and her eyes were glazed a little.

"Jack, let's go to bed."

"I don't want to go to bed. The hell with it."

"Not even with me?"

"Not right now. Jesus Christ, lay off, will you?"

"I just asked you to come to bed."

"I want to sit here."

I looked up at her. She was glaring at me. She was mad as hell. I thought, The hell with it, then.

"What I wanted to tell you," she said. Her voice was flat and level. "When you went out to the store. I saw a car."

"Good for you. Good eyes. Take care of 'em. Precious possession. You'll never know when you need a good pair of eyes. Saw a car—what kind of car?"

"A yellow hardtop." She came closer. "Jack, I swear it was the same car I saw going up and down past the house the other night. The one I told you about."

"Why didn't you tell me before?"

None of it was coming through very well. I fought to clear my head, but it only became worse.

"Jack?"

"Yeah? What now?"

"Who is it owns a yellow car? You know somebody

who owns a yellow hardtop. I think it's a Buick. Who?" She paused and I tried to hold my head up, but I couldn't seem to do it. The hell with it. I was stoned.

"It's that Grace, isn't it," she said. "She owns a yellow hardtop Buick, doesn't she?"

"Yeah. How'd you guess?"

"Now I know why you took so long at the store." I twisted my head up at her, trying to see her. It frightened me deep inside someplace, but I couldn't seem to do anything about it. She blurred and I said, "You're crazy as hell," and everything went away, and I came to, still trying to see her, still trying to say something, only it was daylight.

"Shirley?"

I felt panic. My head was bad. I came to my feet, running, calling her name.

"Shirley. What was that about a yellow car?"

She wasn't in the bedroom.

I ran back across the living room, jumped the pile of money, then damned near fell over the bottles. They were on the floor and they were both empty. The last one had been nearly full, I remembered that. I knew I hadn't drunk it all.

She must have.

And right then I remembered something she'd said a long time ago, it seemed like years. *"When I drink, it makes me go out of my head."*

I went outside. It was misty and chill with morning,

but the sun was coming up over there, a yellow ball. I could feel the faint warmth of the sun.

"Shirley!"

Nothing. She wasn't around. The car was there.

I ran on around the outside of the cabin, and down along the riverbank.

"Shirley?"

There was no sound except the dark purling of the water and the slow wind in the pines. High in the pines. I thought I saw something. I moved on down along the riverbank, calling her name, feeling the panic.

She had said something about a yellow car. Only what? There was one yellow car. Grace's.

"Shirley?"

She didn't answer. I kept moving along the riverbank.

Then I remembered, all right. She had said she'd seen a yellow hardtop Buick when I was over at Wilke's Corners.

And she had said something about knowing it was Grace.

It couldn't have been.

But I wouldn't put anything past Grace.

If it had been Grace, then we had to get out of here. We had to leave right away.

I turned and looked back toward the cabin. Smoke was coming out of the chimney.

"Shirley?"

She didn't answer.

I started back toward the cabin. I don't know what made me run, but I did. I ran back along the river-bank, my feet sliding in the grass and mud. You could hear the black water pulsing against the banks. No other sound. Just my breathing and my feet pounding.

"Shirley?"

The cabin door was open.

I went up on the porch and inside.

She was in front of the fireplace, naked, and she was very drunk. You could see that right away. She didn't stagger, but she was wild-eyed drunk.

The fire was the biggest we'd had, the flames leaping savagely up the chimney. The whole fire-place was a blazing sheet of white flame.

"Shirley?"

"Yes, Jack?"

She stood there in front of the fireplace. I looked over at the shiny white leather suitcase, at the pile of money.

The money wasn't there. I looked around. The money wasn't in sight anywhere. She must have put it in the suitcase.

"Where's the money?" I said.

"I burned it."

"You what!"

"In the fireplace," she said. She turned and pointed at the flames. "In there, Jack. I burned the money. See it? It's burning right now...." I went straight out of my head. I ran to the fire and sprawled across the hearth. I heard myself cursing, and above the cursing I heard the way she laughed. It was something terrible to hear. Then she didn't laugh anymore.

I lay there on my belly, with my face thrust into the flames, scrabbling with my hands. The fire seared my hands and wrists and arms, but I kept snatching and scraping at the flames.

There were a few loose bills strewn around the hearth. But you could see all the rest of them in there, curling and seething and shriveling in the white flames. Crisping and roaring up the chimney flue. The chimney roared and shook, and it was a kind of wild laughter, too.

The heat drove me back. It became more intense.

I turned in a crouch.

"Don't Jack. Don't come near me."

She stood across the room, facing the fire and me, and she had the P-38 in her hand.

I heard myself say it, but it didn't really sound like me at all. "What are you trying to do?"

There was no expression in her voice, and none at all on her face.

"You don't love me," she said. "I know that now. If I'd only known it before, this would never have happened. You don't love me. You love the money."

"You're drunk—you don't know what you're doing."

"You've always loved only the money, and you can't

have the money. Don't you know that? That's how it works, Jack. See?"

"Put down that gun, Shirley."

"No."

I looked at my hands. They were burned badly, and beginning to pain. I was clutching two or three one hundred dollar bills.

"You may as well throw them into the fire with the rest of it," she said. "They're not going to do you any good. You'll never be able to spend them."

"What do you mean?"

"They're coming after us, Jack."

I stood up very slowly, watching her. Her eyes shone, glistening in the fierce light from the fireplace.

"It's the whisky, Shirley. You've done this because you're drunk."

"Maybe. I told you about that, but you kept offering it to me. I warned you. But I was going to do this anyway." She paused. "It came over the radio, Jack. I was right. That woman of yours was here. She followed us—she ran back and got her car and followed us, when we left town that day. Jack—she's been hanging around outside, hiding ever since we got here. Isn't that rich?"

"What are you trying to say?"

"On the radio, while I was burning the money. While you were outside. She told the police, and they're on the way here right now. They didn't say where we were, but they know. We can't get away."

"They can't know."

"She told them. Want to know what she said? She told them the truth, what I suspected, Jack. God, and I loved you—I love you, Jack. I believed in you. She told them you had done this because you loved her. She said you pleaded with her to stay with you, and that you told her you were working a deal where you'd have a lot of money, so you and she could go away together. But when she realized what you had done, she couldn't bear knowing." She took a step toward me. "So she told them. Isn't that just too rich for words, though?"

"You don't believe that."

"Yes. I do believe it, Jack. I've had tiny doubts about you all along. Now I know. You never loved me. It was a way to get money, that's all."

She breathed deeply, and her breasts rose and fell. I saw the way her belly worked. She didn't move that gun, either, and she was just as beautiful as ever, the way she stood there.

"Jack. I've a confession, I want you to know. I had never had a man before. All that was talk. I did it to impress you, because you were the kind of guy you were. I had to be like you—your type, so you'd like me. See?" She took another step toward me. She looked like a savage. "But, I loved you. There's that for you to remember. I really did love you—with every bit of me."

"This is all a lot of—"

"No, Jack. I'm going to kill you. Then I'm going to take my own life, too. Because, that's how I want it. I'll have that much, anyway. I won't go back there and face them, have them look at me with dirty eyes and hear them talk. They'll never know how cheap and false and empty all this was. I'll have that."

"Shirley, listen to me. You're wrought up. You're thinking all wrong. You've got to listen to me. We can get away, if we leave right now. We'd have each other."

"Don't lie to me! No!"

"Shirley, please."

"Jack, Victor was right. You're a son of a bitch. That's all you are. Not a good son of a bitch. A bad son of a bitch. You didn't even take my word on anything. A girl named Veronica Lewis told the police you had her check on Victor's bank account. Was she another hot number, Jack?"

I dropped the bills from my hands. They fluttered to the floor at my feet, on the blankets. My hands burned horribly now and the pain seethed up my arms. I had to reach her, somehow. Maybe I could jump her and get that gun away from her. Because she was *mad!*

"There's lots more," she said. "But why talk about it?"

"Shirley. Honey."

"It's a suicide pact," she said. "That's what it will seem. I've left a note outside, tacked to the door, explaining it. The note is a lie. Like everything else is a lie, since I met you. I told them we burned the money together, because we couldn't have it, and nobody else would. I told them it was a symbol of our love. Isn't that rich, Jack? A symbol of our love. But they'll never know what that really means—how it means emptiness and nothingness. We knew we couldn't escape the law. So we burned the money and killed ourselves. We would be together. We would never return to be sullied by the world."

I stared at her. Then I leaped at her.

She fired. She fired the gun four times, and she hit me three out of the four. I never reached her. I stumbled with the pain in my legs and my side, and sprawled across the blankets. The pain was bad.

"Shirley!"

I was bleeding. I lay there and watched the bleeding and the pain was much worse than I thought pain would ever be. I hadn't thought pain came so swiftly. But it did. It came in blinding white sheets, in hot waves, up and down my body.

I tried to move toward her. I couldn't move. I was too weak and there was too much pain. I lay there looking at her through the reddish film that seemed to spread all through me and I knew that I would die.

She stood looking at me, holding the gun.

Then she stepped softly toward me and knelt on the blankets. Her face was hell to see. She reached out and touched my head, then snatched her hand

away. All I could do was look at her. I kept trying to
say her name.

"Goodbye, Jack. You son of a bitch."

She thought I was dead.

She put the muzzle of that gun to her head and
pulled the trigger. For a long moment she just sat
there with half of her head torn away. I heard myself
scream. It didn't do any good. I couldn't move.

She fell over on me, bleeding and dead.

Somehow I finally got her off me.

Sixteen

I lay there and watched the fire die down, waiting to die myself. I knew that by the time all the flames were gone, I would be gone.

There was no pain now.

I had to look across Shirley's body to see the fire. It leaped across her bare back, and up out of her hair, seething, and it looked as if she were breathing.

She wasn't breathing. She was dead.

It was quiet. As the fire died and died, I gradually came to hear the river again, pulsing endlessly against the banks, and there was the sound of the wind high in the pines. The day became brighter and brighter outside. The sun yellowed the room. And with the sun, the fire died still more, and finally it was nothing but embers.

But I was still all right. Not even bleeding. I was full of lead. My side was ripped open. My left leg was broken. But I was still alive.

I didn't want to be alive.

Then I heard them.

They called the cabin.

"Ruxton! Come out with your hands above, your head."

I couldn't answer them. I could see the gun, still in her hand. It was about two yards away. I tried to reach it, but I couldn't. I tried to crawl to the gun, because then I could kill myself. It was ironic. They would fix me up, if they got to me—fix me up for their kill.

I kept trying to reach the gun. But I couldn't make it.

"Ruxton. We're coming, in!"

I shouted at them. *"No! No!"*

But it was just a sound in my head, it never came from my throat, nothing came past my lips but a whisper.

And then I knew that this was why I had never been able to make it, in all the years of trying, and this was what it had been coming to. Even when I went and took this beautiful gamble. It was simple. Some can make it, others can't. It was that simple.

I couldn't move. I couldn't talk.

I waited.

They finally came across the porch. The door was open. They looked in and saw us lying there. They thought I was dead, too, at first.

An officer of the State Highway Patrol came in. I saw Doctor Miraglia out on the porch. Then a woman screamed, and ran into the room.

"Get her out!" somebody said.

It was Grace. She screamed again, and stood there looking down at me.

They led her back out again, fighting with her every inch of the way.

"Well, Ruxton," Miraglia said. "It's all over, isn't it?"

I just looked at him.

I couldn't figure what they were trying to prove. They all knew what had happened. I even told them the whole story, from the beginning. There was no use holding out. But they kept insisting there must be a trial. It seemed so damned stupid.

They kept me in the hospital, under guard.

Grace came to see me. Don't misunderstand. She didn't come to visit me. She came to *see* me—to stare at me.

She would get a chair and just sit there, staring at me, until they asked her to leave. Every day she did that.

"I'll be there at the end, too, Jack."

She said that every day. She was very nice, because they wouldn't let her stay otherwise. There was nothing I could do.

Yes, that's how it was. Grace, she was always burning. Then Shirley and I began burning. And then the money burned. And now there was time to burn.

Then, after there was no more time, they would burn me.

Don't Let the Mystery End Here.
Try These Other Great Books From
HARD CASE CRIME!

Hard Case Crime brings you gripping, award-winning crime fiction
by best-selling authors and the hottest new writers in the field.
Find out what you've been missing:

The CONFESSION
by DOMENIC STANSBERRY
WINNER OF THE EDGAR® AWARD!

She was young, beautiful...and dead!

Jake Danser has it all: a beautiful wife, a house in the California
hills, and a high-profile job as a forensic psychologist. But he's
also got a mistress. And when she's found strangled to death
with his necktie, the police show up at his door. Now it's up to
Jake to prove he didn't do it. But how can he, when all the
evidence says he did?

As Jake's life crumbles around him, he races to find proof of his
innocence. And with every step, the noose is tightening...

PRAISE FOR THE BOOKS OF DOMENIC STANSBERRY:

"Fascinating, beautifully written...an enviable achievement."
— San Francisco Chronicle

"A murky, moody slice of noir."
— Kirkus Reviews

"A compelling and incredibly dark modern noir shocker."
— Publishers Weekly on *The Confession*

Available now at your favorite bookstore.
For more information, visit
www.HardCaseCrime.com